BANG

Tori Ross

CONTENTS

Author's Note

If you're here because you like my romantic comedy and think this will be anything like *The Pipe Cleaner*, turn around. You're in the wrong place. But if you think this book is like *Copper*, which was my first romantic suspense, you're also in for a bit of shock.

This book is darker. Know that going in. You don't NEED to read *Copper* before reading this. If you can accept things as they come onto the page, you don't really need to go back, but reading the first book helps understand the side characters of Lucy and Aaron, and it will especially help when Kyle gets to the epilogue here. But again, it's not necessary.

Grab a stiff drink. Beer. Wine. Whatever you like.

Most importantly, buckle the fuck up and enjoy. Don't think too hard about this. I am absolutely aware that every single character in this book needs multiple sessions with a mental health professional, but this is fiction.

I can't believe I have to write this, but you never know these days. **Do not do anything my characters do, OK?** We're just going to roll with it and enjoy the sweet stench of made-up vigilante street justice without hurting anyone in real life.

Everything is made up. For example, names are all random here. I'm super sorry if your name is really Mark Ricord, Daniel Martin, Troy Acox, or Jake Portsmith. Hell, I'm kind of sorry about using Kyle Mitchell and Cheryl Briggs. Readers should know that those names are just names, and nothing is based on real people. So don't go harassing anyone.

Lastly, if you need to talk to someone because you are thinking about harming yourself or others, please call 988 in the US or check with your local suicide hotline if in another country. If you're cutting or self-harming, please also call that number. They can get you to someone who can help.

Content Warnings: Torture, violent death, off-screen castration, on-screen ear removal, a heel shot to the eye for those squeamish about eye stuff, memories of SA, memories of domestic violence, memories of childhood abuse, present domestic violence, masochism, and...blood during sexy time.

No animals are harmed, and I know people will be worried about the boys as soon as you soon them, but no children are harmed at any point. Only the deserving and guilty are dealt with in my world.

Other than that, let's agree that anything is on the table, OK?

And not everything is as it seems...

Let's fucking go.

CHAPTER 1

Cheryl

Breathe in through the nose.

Breathe out through the mouth.

My therapist back in Minnesota always told me to name five things you can see, three things you feel, two things you can hear, and one thing you can smell. To be fair, my therapist was an absolute nut who believed anxiety and depression from past trauma could be cured by Jesus and a good jog in the sunshine, but it's worth a try at this point.

I close my eyes, squeezing them shut, only to open them because I kind of need them to do that whole thing about seeing something. My vision is hazy, it always is when the panic attacks come, but I focus on the stripper pole metal under my right hand. It's extra shiny tonight.

I see pink neon lights. My bright blue nail polish shines up from my toes, and I even give them a wriggle. A minuscule tube of hand chalk leans against the mirror behind me. Women are in front of me on the other poles around the room. They aren't men. I'm safe here. Safe from the grabbing or even the slaps to the face that were so common at the cheap club in Duluth. When I moved here to the Chicago suburbs after the twins started school, it was better, but I still had to do things I didn't want to do.

Feel.

I wiggle my painted toes in my stripper shoes. The pole is cold under my hand. My new fake lashes that were on clearance at Walmart itch. I always forget I'm slightly allergic to the glue.

Hear.

The women chat excitedly and laugh at each other as they test the martini spins I've taught them. The music blares from the speakers Lucy just installed.

Smell.

Lucy's a big fan of cleaning the poles and floor after every single class. Bleach still lingers in the air. The scent mixes with the tea tree oil diffuser in the corner. Lucy doesn't like her pole workout club smelling too much like a hospital.

I've worked here since she opened. I still work at her cousin's strip club on weekend nights and pull a random day shift while the kids are at school, but when Lucy opened the workout club teaching pole routines and chair dances to bored housewives, I jumped at the chance to teach classes a few days a week. Sure, I'm not getting tips from men in pit-stained suits, but she pays a decent enough wage to cut back my lap dance time.

My heart palpitations slow as I ground myself.

I'm safe here. Safe from the twins' father who sexually assaulted me eleven years ago when I was only eighteen and has fought me for custody since, wanting the children my family pretty much forced me to have. I work for my ex-coworker, Lucy, whose fiancé is the local sheriff. He's here all the time, bringing her lunch or disappearing into the cleaning closet with her in the middle of the afternoon for way longer than the time it takes for her to find a new roll of paper towels. The sheriff walking us to our cars most nights means safety for me. He's a cop, and I'm normally distrustful of the police, but his love for my boss and his calm demeanor make being here the safest I've felt in a long time. Not much ruffles Sheriff Aaron Dwyer.

"When you're done with the spin out and reach the floor, you can add a saucy backward somersault and sexy crawl. It drives them nuts," I say, pasting a smile on my face.

If I'm good at anything, it's pretending and faking my way through the panic. As long as I live, I'll never get over that I now help middle-aged women do backward somersaults for the first time in thirty years and teach them doe eyes to entice their husbands before a well-timed blow job. Life is often surprising.

I check the clock on the wall just as the last song on the beginning pole class playlist wraps up. "That's all for today, ladies! If you need a chalk stick or some gear, Lucy's up front."

The women file out, all clucking and smiling about wherever they're going next. A bar for margaritas? Home to their husbands and children? It must be nice having friends you can go to the gym with. I wouldn't know. After the shit storm that was my early adulthood, I never had the chance to make many friends. I work. I go home. I help my twin boys, who are going into fourth grade, with homework. I make some kind of dinner, which is usually waffles and yogurt with a banana, and then I crash out. That is, if I'm not on the pole that night.

The only friends I have are people like Lucy, but I'm hesitant to call her my friend since she's technically my boss now, and I know she only hired me because we worked together at the club. I was hired because she trusts I know my way around a pole, not for my sparkling personality. We were never close, but she's secure in my ability to teach climbs and spins. In my world, bosses aren't our friends. A few girls at the club are friendly enough, especially after what we went through a few months ago with Murphy Beckett, a local drug dealer and trafficker, making us move his fentanyl for him. But he's dead and gone, and my coworkers and I haven't really talked about it since. The conversations in the back room at the club now center around who took someone's lipstick and if anyone has double-sided tape to fix the Velcro on their rippable panties.

I gather my gear and head out to the lobby as fast as I can, knowing full well that Lucy's anxious to get home to Aaron. She'll clean the room and then head out.

"No Aaron tonight?" I ask, approaching the counter lit with pink neon lights and a few potted plants Lucy likes. I squint after being in the dim pole room.

She shakes her head, and a strand of her auburn hair falls out of her ponytail. "He had Ruby's musical at school. It's something that the class does every year."

"You didn't go?"

She looks down and bites her lip. "He invited me. Ruby did, too. I just feel like I don't fit sometimes. That seems like a mom thing, right?"

I lean against the counter and frown. "Lucy, you're marrying Ruby's dad. You'll be a stepmom. Stepmoms go places like that, even if the mom shows up. You don't have that problem since Aaron's wife died a couple years ago."

"I know. I need to find my place. I'm just floundering since Aaron and I got engaged. It's real, you know? I can hide behind work. After what my first husband put me through, I'm scared to fuck up or even blink wrong, even though Aaron would never hurt me. I'm also scared the girls will think I'm trying too hard at replacing their mom, and then Aaron will think I'm not trying hard enough."

"I think you should talk to him. He may be a cop, but I don't hold that against him."

I tap the counter but don't wait for her to respond. I need to get home to my boys, and I give Lucy a wave before heading out the door, the bell above the door tinkling in my wake.

It's dark in the parking lot, and I miss Aaron. He usually walks us out. I grip my keys between my fingers like they taught us in high school health class. My heartbeat hasn't really slowed to normal since the panic attack, but it speeds up even more as I look behind me and squint toward the dumpster. I don't know what I think I'll see. A bear? That's not really a thing in the Chicago suburbs. A coyote? More likely. The wind blows, and the metal on the dumpster creaks like someone is lifting the lid.

"It's just the fucking wind. Get a grip," I mumble under my breath and walk faster to my car.

I should have taken my heels off so I can walk faster. I usually take them off right after class, but I just didn't this time. I'm so used to eight-inch hooker heels that I often forget they aren't sneakers. I know that sounds insane. It sounds crazy in my head as I look down at the bright red heels that practically match my hair color and give a small smile.

I'm suddenly jerked back by my hair, and I drop my keys nearby, noting the clattering sound in my panic. The sound of the metal is deafening in the silent parking lot. I scrabble to remove whatever is in my hair, and it takes me a few seconds for my brain to connect the dots that someone has a hunk of my hair wrapped around their fist.

"Hi, baby. Nice to see you," a familiar voice coos into my ear, and I quickly jerk my head forward and then back, cracking my boys' father square in the fucking teeth.

He lets go, and I quickly spin to face him, my hands out. I'm still in shock and don't think to block the slap that soon stings my face. When Daniel hit me in the past, he was usually careful to make sure it was open-handed to not leave marks, and this time is no different. Stinging pain floods my face, and I almost fall at the force of it. Thankfully, I stay upright.

"What do you want?" I ask, my voice loud. If he thinks I'll draw attention to him, maybe he'll leave.

Lucy will come out.

Lucy will come out.

Daniel never hits in front of other people.

But Lucy doesn't come, and Daniel's hand grips my throat, lifting me off the ground just enough that I'm on my tiptoes as he forces me to look into his face. He smiles, and I wish I could knock his perfect teeth out.

He hasn't changed much in the years since the date rape. His hair recedes, and he combs it back like a car salesman. I can smell the wax pomade or some other hair product as he holds me close, leering. His shoulders are broader, and he's wider around the chest than when we were late teens. As I study his familiar face with his chiseled jaw and high cheekbones, I notice a new scar near his hairline and find myself hoping a girl got in a good shot with a beer bottle.

"I just want to say hello, Cheryl. Can't I say hello to the mother of my children?"

"Your way of saying hello is fucked up. Why are you two states from home?"

"Why wouldn't I be when your lawyer filed a brief to take me back to court for more child support? I think that's something we should chat about."

"Your chats are bullshit, Daniel."

He laughs and rears back his head. At first, I flinch, thinking he'll head butt me, but warm spit suddenly oozes down my face, sticking to my eyelashes. It's not the first time he's spit in my face. The first time was when I was in the maternity ward after giving birth and had the nurses take the babies to the nursery to keep them from Daniel taking them while I was still trying to walk right. From experience, I also know if I react negatively, I'll just get more pain or humiliation.

Even with the threat of more violence, I swallow and take a deep breath. "You've paid the same amount since they were born. That was over ten years ago, Daniel. That's not accounting for inflation and the fact you've been promoted twice in that time. I don't think it's unrealistic to give me a few extra bucks for your kids."

He lets go of my throat, and I prepare for the slap I know is coming. When it comes, this time on the other cheek, my legs are braced to stay upright again. I'm getting good at being beat on.

He grips my hair again and pulls so hard that I'm forced into a back bend to not lose a hunk of it.

"Look at those trashy shoes on your feet. How much of my child support goes to that?"

"I paid for these out of my tips, asshole. I buy food and pay my rent with what you send. I think you'd be fine with the boys having a roof over their heads." I don't mention that I pay for most of the food in the house and most of the rent with my body. The shoes are a necessary business expense to earn rent.

He pulls harder, and I wince. I'm halfway to the ground, and he hovers over me, his eyes dark. I know that look.

No.

The word rattles in my head like a banshee scream. Not again. Not this time. Not ever. Not here in this parking lot. Not even in the depths of fucking hell.

His hands move to his fly, and he unbuttons his pants. "If I'm going to pay more, I'm going to get my money's worth from the whore who's taking it."

Blazing heat moves up my spine. I bite my lip to stop it from trembling. The last time this happened, I cried. I cried and yelled until he put a sock in my mouth to shut me up. But I was also eighteen the last time it happened, and the world has made me hard over the years. I'm a dancer with better flexibility, stronger legs, and have had to fight off my fair share of dickheads at the club. This time, he'll need more than his bare hands and a sock to contain my rage. I'm no longer the helpless young woman I once was.

I kick out, sweeping his knee out from under him. He falls, but his hand stays in my hair, and I go down with him. We're both in a jumble on the ground, and I pry his fingers away from my hair, wincing as I lose a few strands in the process. Once free, I crabwalk backward until Daniel grabs my leg and pulls me back to him as my fingers scramble against the gravel.

"Lucy!" I scream.

Maybe if Lucy comes out, Daniel will run. I've never known him to hurt anyone but me. I'm his preferred punching bag in life. Otherwise, he desperately tries to appear nice and innocent to every other human on the planet. He'd clean himself up and tell Lucy I attacked him.

Lucy is probably running a mop over the pole room with her earbuds in and has no idea I'm fighting for my life. The idea of Lucy dancing to music in a building twenty yards away while my ex assaults or even kills me in a parking lot is surreal. I can't go out like this.

Self-defense? I never took it. Why didn't I take it?

Memories of an old episode of *Oprah* my mother watched when I was a child fill my head. Really? The last thing I'm going to think about is Oprah Winfrey as Daniel grabs my leg and twists so I'm forced to my stomach on the wet asphalt. My face hits gravel. Shit. That won't get me any tips at the club until it heals.

Legs. Women are stronger in the legs. That's what Oprah's guest, who was there to show women basic self-defense moves, said about being attacked. I remember a woman dropping to the ground and kicking the shit out of her assailant. At the time, I thought it was stupid. Why wouldn't you just run? Doesn't it take time to heave yourself from the ground and get away?

But if you're already helpless on the ground...

I kick out and hit him square in the chin with the ball of my foot.

"Fucking bitch!" he growls. He holds on to one leg like hell, but I still have one free, even as he tries to get an arm around it.

His hands scramble at my boy shorts like he wants them off. Is he really still trying to go for it after all this?

I hurt him with the chin shot, though. It's the first time I've ever fought back against him instead of cowering against the wall, letting him box me in, and doing whatever he wants. I actually struck back. He's called me a bitch before, but somehow there's more meaning now. I've actually done something to be a bitch in his eyes. How dare I kick his precious face?

I lift my free leg again and strike, this time hitting him in the chin with my heel....that goes straight up into his chin.

Gasping at the shock of my own power, I watch as blood streams from his chin and slowly pull the spiked heel out of Daniel's face with a squishing sound. He covers the spot I kicked, letting go of my leg and putting pressure on the blood leaking from his face. The red liquid seeps through his fingers, and I know I got him good.

Either way, I'm free, and I scramble backward, my eyes and mouth all wide in shock that I did that to him.

"Bith, I'm gon ki you," he says, glaring. Did I get the bottom of his tongue? Is that why the words aren't coming out correctly?

When he lets go of his chin, blood is everywhere. It runs down his front, over his neck, and drips to the asphalt. There's no hiding this if someone checks the area.

Again.

That's the only word that runs through my head. Kick him again, this time the temple.

I scoot to the side, and my legs wobble as I attempt to stand, partly from fear of what I've done and partly from rage. As soon as get leverage, I lift my leg again and kick. He bats it away and runs his fingernails down my legs. He doesn't have long nails like a woman, but the scratches still hurt.

I kick again and find his head. This time, the heel connects with his fucking temple.

His body stills in shock, and his eyes widen as I scurry to get into a better position above him, and I work to keep from falling into a heap. Blood gushes out his temple and his chin, but the temple strike wasn't nearly as deep. He looks up at me with anger, and I know then that I need to make it so he doesn't get up again. I'll be dead. If this man stands again, he'll kill me, even with a damaged noggin and mouth.

He shakes a little like he's having a seizure and rolls to his stomach. He tries to get up but crawls after me as I take two steps back.

"You mother fucker!" I scream.

I don't even care if Lucy comes out right at this second. I can explain. Something about Lucy that I can never quite put my finger on tells me she'd understand, even help me.

"Why can't you just me alone or be civil?"

I kick at him again, and he doesn't block it. He's probably in shock because he only stares at the ground and the blood oozing onto it from his body. He pants like a fucking dog as the aim of my kick is off, and I only hit him in the shoulder.

"Cun," he says.

I bend at the waist and study him. "Oh, can we not pronounce cunt for some reason? I wonder why. It felt good driving my heel into your chin, you mother fucker!" It didn't feel good. It was disgusting, but who gets to taunt now? I'm going to revel in it. "Gee, that's too bad about your face."

I've been so angry about this mother fucker for so long. Date rape. Forced to have my kids. I don't exactly regret them. I love my boys, but I never would have chosen this life for myself. After I had them, I had to fight for child support, which I didn't get much of because his lawyers were better. But he still wanted more custody. There was always a fight in court or physically. He didn't leave bruises, and I had no proof. For the last ten years, I've had to co-parent with my rapist, and that does things to a woman.

Angry heat fills my body, and it moves from my ears and all the way to the tips of my toes. I throw my head back, taking my eyes off him while he's attacking me for the first time in my life. Why? Because I know I have the upper hand for the first time.

I grit my teeth and growl as I look up at the quarter moon. I roll my neck and my shoulders like I just grew a new skin and I'm trying it on. Even the air smells better, cleaner somehow. I can't explain what happens to my lungs when I take a deep breath, but I can only imagine it's what a pneumonia victim feels like when their lungs are finally empty and they can take deep breaths again.

This. Ends. Tonight. My entire pathetic doormat existence dies here in this parking lot.

I lift my legs for another kick, and I have a split second to think about where I want to aim it. I let my body decide, finally trusting myself. No more guessing about what needs to be done in life. No more apologies for things I didn't do. No more bowing to people who don't deserve another glance. I bring my foot down right onto his neck and grind my fucking heel into it to make the biggest hole possible.

He shrieks like a little girl and hits the ground, falling out of his crawl position. His fingers scrabble against my foot as he tries to fight, but I must have struck something important here. When I remove my heel, it makes a terrible squishing sound again, and blood pumps out of his neck like a horror movie. It coats my legs and feet.

Again.

No fear or looking over my shoulder for him or his shitty lawyers anymore. No more worrying if the next time he shows up for visitation is the last time I see my boys. Daniel has threatened more than once to take them away where I'll never find them.

Daniel flips over, and I go for the eye for one last kick.

He stops moving after my heel pushes through his left eye. For the first time since I started kicking him, I'm afraid to retract my heel and consider just leaving it in his eye and taking the damn shoe off. I go with that. I don't care what he's done to me. I cannot pull my shoe out and risk the eyeball coming with it.

Quickly, I unbuckle my shoe at the ankle as Daniel's body shakes under me. I once cut the head off a snake in my garage, and it shook and writhed for a minute after its head came off. Are humans the same? I've never killed anyone before, but I watch as he trembles and his fingers twitch for thirty seconds. You cannot tell me Daniel will get up from a neck strike, a chin jab, and two head stabs. I watch for what seems like minutes as the twitching moves to different parts of the body. His eyes. His feet. I swear I see his nose wriggle before he goes suddenly still and a small stream of water moves across the pavement under his butt.

"What in the actual fuck?" a voice says behind me, and I close my eyes.

"I can explain, Lucy," I mumble, grimacing through clenched teeth.

She's silent for ten seconds as I look down at Daniel, my hands on my hips and still not turning to face Lucy. I'm scared of what I'll see when I face her. It's safe to say I'm probably fired, but I'm not sure what kind of facial expression one puts on for their boss who just found their employee standing over a dead body in the parking lot. Do I smile? Look mean so she won't cross me, even though I'd never hurt her?

"Jesus Christ, is your stripper heel clean through his eye?" Lucy asks.

"Yes, ma'am," I whisper. "I'm sorry. This is Daniel." I gesture to the man on the ground. "Daniel, this is my boss, Lucy. She'd shake your hand, I'm sure, but you're busy dying and all."

"You know this man?" she asks.

I finally turn to face her and find a surprisingly neutral expression on my boss's face. There's a hint of curiosity there, judging by the scowl on her forehead, but I don't see horror or fear. Only concern.

"He's my ex. The boys' father." I rub my neck. "He was waiting for me and attacked me." Silence as she stares at him on the ground. "I guess he was mad about me asking for an increase in child support, huh?" I chuckle, even though nothing about this is funny. "I had to... improvise," I say, pointing at my bare foot. I cross my fingers she can see the red mark where he slapped me and my messy hair so she can form her own opinion on what happened.

Lucy takes two tentative steps forward and cranes her neck. "Didn't want to pull the shoe out?"

"Nope. I can't stand the idea that an eyeball would come with it. Apparently, that's my line when killing my ex."

"Everyone has a line." Lucy inhales deeply and looks around the parking lot. "Clean shot, though. Well done on positioning."

"You're not mad about this?" I ask.

She bites her bottom lip, thinking. She takes four steps and looks down the street at our nearest neighboring business, a taco joint with cameras in their lot. "Probably not close enough for them to get a good shot. The bushes between our properties kind of cover some things, too. Not like they'd rat on us anyway. They don't want attention brought to them with some family members from Mexico working in the place, and we're going to leave them the fuck out of this." She looks around. "Open your trunk."

"What?" I ask.

"Well, we can't just leave the bastard here with a shoe in his eye!" She points to Daniel. "Open your trunk."

I take my other shoe off so I can walk and then shuffle over to my car on bare feet. I search for my keys, pick them up with shaky fingers, and take two tries to press the button for the trunk. Once the trunk is open, I walk back to her, taking small steps on the painful gravel and watching for broken beer bottle glass that always seems to be around.

"Help me get him in your car. You lift the bloody half since you're the one who did the damage."

I bend and lift Daniel's shoulders as blood still pours out of him. Who knew people had this much blood inside of them? I sure didn't. If he wasn't dead from the strikes, bleeding out would do it.

Lucy suddenly drops her end of him, and I tumble forward, almost falling. "What the fuck?"

She turns and heads toward the door of her business. "We need trash bags to line the trunk. Otherwise, he'll bleed all over it. I have some cleaning gloves, too."

Lucy goes inside for a few minutes while I wait in the parking lot, tapping my foot and wondering if I should drag Daniel behind the dumpster in case someone happens to be lost and pulls into the parking lot to turn around or something. What would I do then? Smile and wave?

Eventually, she comes back and silently lines my trunk with plastic sheeting she must have left over after painting the place a few months ago. She even has duct tape with her and tapes the sheeting to the edge of the trunk, making a bowl-like plastic protection for my car. On top of that, she lays four trash bags down and two old towels.

"There," she says. "Now we can get him in. I'll hose off the asphalt and pour some bleach over the top of that. I got some new scrubbers that should get most of it. The parking lot will be good as new."

Lucy goes back to Daniel's feet and squares her legs before squatting to lift. I can't help but think about my retail job in high school where we had an entire training session on team lifts and using our legs. I guess that information is finally coming in handy.

"He's a heavy mother fucker, that's for sure," Lucy says, grunting a little as she lifts.

"He was always bulky. Lifted a lot."

"Ugh. I hate muscular jerks. It makes dealing with this harder."

"What's harder?"

She blushes at the question. How does Lucy know muscular dead men are harder to deal with?

"You're abnormally calm about this," I say when she doesn't answer.

Blood from Daniel's head and neck runs down my legs to my ankles. Maybe Lucy can go inside and get me some wipes. I'm not sure I have enough baby wipes in the car. I usually carry them for the boys' sticky hands if they eat in the car, but they sure don't make this kind of mess.

Lucy's eyes meet mine for the first time since she found me hovering over Daniel. Her normally dark eyes are even darker, but an eyebrow is raised like she has a question or possible secret. "Shit happens, honey. Shit happens to men like this sometimes."

"Should we call Aaron?" I ask.

We heave Daniel into my trunk, trying twice to get him all the way in. Lucy has to put a knee under Daniel's butt as we push and roll him over the bumper more than we lift, and we both watch as my small sedan sags with his weight.

"No. Let's leave him out of this."

I run my hands through my hair and stare into the car as Lucy's hand hovers over the lid of my trunk. She crosses her legs at the ankle and leans against the car like she's waiting for me to make a decision. Panic or not panic.

I've panicked a fuck ton in my life, and I choose not to do it today.

"I can't hide this, Lucy," I say, waving toward Daniel. His non-stabbed eye is closed, and I've only seen him angry or leering over me my whole life. This is the first time he seems at peace. Maybe I did him a favor.

"There's a dead guy in my trunk. Correction, the father of my children is in my trunk. I've fought him in court for a long time. The system isn't going to believe me that he attacked me. They'll only see..." My voice trails off, and I clear my throat to remove the husky fear from my voice. "They just won't believe me. They're not going to believe a stripper over a guy like Daniel."

"I know. That's why we're going to stay calm. This isn't your fault. It was self-defense."

"That's why we should tell Aaron. He'd believe me." Why am I pushing for him to get involved in this more than Lucy? Shouldn't she already be calling him for help?

"He may, but it still has to go into the legal system, and you'll have to prove self-defense in front of a grand jury. Was this guy rich? He looks rich. Those are really nice pants."

"Typical coddled frat guy. Dad's a big lawyer up in Minnesota."

Lucy cringes. "That's not good. I was hoping you were going to say he grew up poor and already has a record a mile long."

"Nope. If anything, I'm the one with a record." I squeeze my eyes shut and try not to panic over my failed attempts at shoplifting when I was eighteen and the time I got caught with two ounces of marijuana before it was legalized. I'm the one with the rap sheet. Even if Aaron says self-defense, Lucy's right. Questions will be raised. Daniel's father is a powerful attorney and may know someone here. Since this abuse and my relationship with Daniel has spanned two states and a Minnesota custody dispute, even the police response may not be up to Aaron. It may end up on the FBI's desk, and I'd certainly be fucked there since I'm not a white male with lots of cash.

The white male with lots of cash is currently bleeding out on trash bags in my trunk.

I still want to believe Aaron would help. "Are you sure we shouldn't call?"

"That's actually a small problem for me," she says, pinching the bridge of her nose like this is a big inconvenience.

"What kind of problem?"

"The problem about how I promised Aaron I'd never get violent with men again. I'm not going into details, but you remember how I asked for a little of that fentanyl you were being forced to push months back?"

"Yeah..." I draw the word out and squint.

"Someone well-deserving met a sticky end on that one. I won't explain or mention it again. Understand? Not one word. We didn't have this conversation. I thought you'd already figured it out anyway."

My mouth opens, but I can't really respond. I have no idea what I'd say. Did Lucy kill someone? I thought she just got the fentanyl to give it to another client or dealer that came through the strip club. I thought she was caught up in the blackmail like we all were.

"I promised Aaron I wouldn't be involved in anything like this again unless our family is at risk, and I won't go back on that promise. I'm going to help you because I know what it's like to be abused and scared, but that's where our relationship on this ends. I'm going to help you clean this up because another woman helped me once, and we'll never speak of it again. It'll be business as usual. Aaron may not see this as me keeping my promises. I want him left out of it just like I'm going to walk away from this and erase it from my mind after I drag the hose over here and get this fucker's blood out of my lot." She curls her lip as she looks back at the pavement.

"What do I do with the body in my trunk?"

Lucy taps her fingers on my car before sighing and pulling her phone out of the side pocket of her leggings. She dials a number, and I hear the phone ringing tone from five feet away. When a woman picks up the phone, there's a muffled greeting like we woke the woman, and Lucy blows out a breath of what could be relief or could be the fact that she doesn't necessarily want to talk to this person. Maybe both.

Lucy bites her cheek for a full two seconds before beginning to speak.

"Hey, Ellen. I know I'm clean out of favors, but I need a favor."

Chapter 2

Kyle...Three Month Later

Why does she keep crossing and uncrossing her legs? That's a damning tell that she's nervous and hiding something. Not that I'd care if she's nervous since most people are when they're called down to the county police station for routine questions. Even if it's about something they saw that didn't personally involve them, people simply don't like talking to the police. Honestly, I don't blame them.

I shouldn't even be conducting the questioning, but Coleson isn't here and Dwyer recused himself since Cheryl Briggs is his fiancée's employee. He thought it would be too weird and also look bad if Daniel Martin's family wanted to dig into it. They'd flag it as fishy, and Sheriff Aaron Dwyer doesn't like fishy, especially not for the last few months. You'd think, with him getting married soon and all, he'd be in a great mood and like a teacher who doesn't assign homework on the weekend. In reality, he's been strict and grumpy at work if anyone questions the rules. Everything is by the book down to the letter.

Gee, it's like he's making up for something. A fuck-up along the way? Worried something will bite him in the ass?

I avert my eyes from the very long legs covered in black fishnet stockings. I work to keep my tongue in my mouth and not lick my lips like I've done when I've seen her in those same fishnets at the club. She's fucking beautiful, and she's been one of my favorites there since we staked out the club for info on Murphy Beckett. Not that I've approached her. I admire from afar.

Dear God, those legs.

"Take your time," I urge. "Think hard. When was the last time you talked to Daniel Martin?"

She taps her red, manicured fingers on my desk and leans back in her chair. Her eyes move to the ceiling like she's thinking. "Four months ago. Maybe a bit longer."

"And what was that conversation like?" I ask, typing her words into my laptop and trying not to remember the shade of pink of her nipples. They're bright pink like her bottom lip she's currently chewing.

Her eyes flick back to me, and she furrows her brow. I want to take my index finger and drag it down the bridge of her nose to rub out any pain or anxiety she has. There's something hard-as-nails about her. But there's also something soft in there. Something broken and scratching at civilized society while trying to survive. I see it. She's also more fascinating and beautiful up close.

"Do I need a lawyer, Sheriff?"

"Not unless you want one. We're just hoping you can help us find Daniel Martin. Any information you have will be helpful." I pause tapping my tablet for a second. "I'm not Sheriff Dwyer. You know who that is. You work with his future wife."

"Is Aaron the only sheriff in town?"

I smile at her innocent question. "There's usually only one in the county since he's elected. I'm a deputy."

"Isn't that like a peon?" she asks, leaning forward in her chair.

"No, ma'am," I lie, even though I'm low on the totem pole around here. It suits me fine, though. Everyone loves a bumbling deputy who brings in cream-filled donuts on Tuesday morning when Aaron's assistant, Bertie, doesn't bring a snack. Look at the character of Dewey in the *Scream* franchise, for fuck's sake. People underestimate you and don't put a lot on your shoulders when they think you're the sweet, loveable dude. My goal around this joint is to do my job and go the fuck home.

"It was the usual type of conversation," Cheryl answers with a one-shouldered shrug. "I wanted more child support because I get enough for half a cart of groceries right now. It's not enough, and I need to support my boys. He said no. He picked the boys up and took them somewhere. Jonah said they had ice cream and went to the park. Daniel brought them back at the usual time. He backed out of the driveway, and I politely waved from the porch. I used all five fingers instead of the one I wanted to use since the boys were there."

"Jonah is your son?" I ask, typing.

"I have twins. He's the oldest by four minutes. Jonah and Jordan."

"Do your sons have a good relationship with their father?"

"You can't be serious in thinking my sons have something to do with Daniel missing?"

I smile. "No, ma'am. We're just trying to figure out if he's attached to them and would normally make contact. We need to know if it's unusual for him not to connect with them."

I don't type the part about her automatically jumping to something happening to cause no contact between Daniel Martin and her or his family in Minnesota. I'm not out to press this woman too much, especially since I haven't felt butterflies like the ones currently fluttering in my stomach for a long time. Is this what it was like when Aaron Dwyer was trying to figure out what was going on in the club Lucy worked at several months ago? Because the only thing I want to do right now is put down my stupid report and pull this woman next to me. Maybe sit on the couch with some Chinese food and watch a comedy. Something light to take away the obvious darkness in her eyes.

"My sons see their father when he shows up. They don't complain about it, but I wouldn't necessarily say they skip in excitement," she says, interrupting my thoughts of cozy home life with a feisty redhead. "They've had the same setup their whole lives as far as custody goes. Daniel loves them. Whatever issues he and I had, our kids weren't the problem."

"Is it normal for him to have no contact with his family for months?" I ask.

I know it's not normal. He's a daily caller to his father. I certainly don't want to needle her, but I need to see if she loses her cool.

"You'd have to ask them. It's my impression he got along fine with them, but I wasn't exactly privy to their family party and holiday schedule, if you know what I mean, Mr..."

"Mitchell. Deputy Kyle Mitchell. Please call me Kyle."

She blinks, and her eyes move slowly enough to look like she's batting her eyes at me. I certainly don't mind. I try not to stare at her beautiful almond-shaped eyes with long lashes.

I clear my throat and tear my eyes away from her. It's hard. "Is it normal for *you* not to have contact with him?" I ask, looking down at my report again.

She bites her lip and looks at her feet while tapping her sneakers on the floor like she enjoys the sound. Tip tap. Tip tap. I obviously caught her on the way to work. Her skirt is short. Her fishnets aren't something you wear to the grocery store, but she's paired them with old, retro Pumas. I wouldn't put on the shoes with heels the length of my dick until I got to work either.

Great. Now I'm thinking about this woman and my dick.

"It's not normal. He comes over monthly or meets me halfway. The boys get one week in Minnesota over the Christmas break, and they spend two weeks at their grandparents' house in the summer. We have to text often to work out visitation since it's ordered for me to do so and allow access to the kids. But it's also not something I'd think twice about if I didn't hear from him. I just figured he hadn't texted or seen the boys because he found a new hot thing that didn't like kids. We were civil in front of the boys. I let them see him because I'll be in contempt if I don't. That's it."

"You don't like him."

"No, sir. I don't."

"Does he hurt you?"

She snort laughs and looks around the bullpen. It's mostly empty except for another deputy sipping coffee and listening to something through headphones three desks away. Even the televisions on the wall that are usually tuned to Chicago news are off.

"Do you know what's shitty about our society, Kyle?"

I raise an eyebrow and subconsciously lean forward. "No, ma'am."

That's a fucking lie. I know exactly what's wrong with society. I've seen it. I kind of want to see what she says, though.

"Daniel Martin was my blind date for my prom. Yeah, I had a blind date to my prom. It was supposed to be fun. One of my friends had a boyfriend who was Daniel's best friend. But it wasn't very much fun at the end of the night when he held me down and raped me. I didn't know what it was then, but I know now. Back then, I thought it was my fault for drinking a little, wearing too short of a dress, and attending a late-night party with him." She inhales deeply. She probably doesn't tell people about it often. "I also blamed myself six weeks later when the stick turned pink."

God damn. I had an inkling Daniel Martin is a douchebag, but I didn't have rapist on the bingo card.

"Word gets around when you're that age and everyone knows your business." She shrugs. "It got back to him that I was pregnant. It also got back to his daddy, who made sure I didn't get an abortion. His parents told my parents. Everyone knew each other from the country club and were big political donors. An abortion would look bad." She slides down in her seat, and I can almost imagine the scared eighteen-year-old she was. "My mom guilted me into having the boys and giving them to Daniel. I was called a slut and a whore. I was told I shamed my family, but that it would be more shameful to abort if someone found out. I should have just told her the truth that he raped me, but knowing my mother, it would have been my fault for wearing too short of a dress to prom or it would be God's will. I'd heard it all my life, which is probably why I thought it was my fault in the first place."

"I'm sorry," I whisper.

I jiggle my leg under the desk. Rape stories are hard for me and the worst part of my job. My face burns with angry heat, and my heart speeds up. I blink and focus on Cheryl's mouth to keep from going down a road of very dark thoughts.

"To my mother, everything is God's will, even rape. I had the babies because Daniel, his parents, my parents, and even the fucking priest pressured me. I saw my boys come out of me and..." She shakes her head as her voice trails off. She clears her throat and rolls her shoulders, working up the strength to keep going. "Once I saw them and saw they were boys, there was no way I was going to just hand them to Daniel and his family for them to raise just like Daniel." She curls her fingers, forming a makeshift cup, and presses her hand to her chest. "I felt like I had to protect them, you know? Raise them to be kinder to women. I want my boys to be good men."

"I'm sure you're a great mom to them."

She looks up with a furrowed brow. Perhaps she's surprised that I agree with her. "I am. I also don't know anything about where Daniel is. There was nothing unusual about him the last time I saw him."

"Nothing?"

She looks at a spot behind me and bites her cheek. It's a gesture some people do to keep from laughing, but she could be thinking. "His eye looked a little red."

I type that into my report, but I'm sure that's nothing. Sounds like he rubbed it the wrong way. Even if someone is high, both eyes are usually red. Hell, maybe he had pinkeye.

"Are there any friends that he may have had that you can think that the family wouldn't know about? A girlfriend your sons mentioned?"

"No. I don't know the names of anyone he dates, and he didn't bring them around the boys that I know of."

There's literally nothing to go on here.

"Do you know of anyone who would want to hurt him?"

She leans over my desk on her elbows and looks at me, blinking twice. A silver necklace with an emerald at the end of the chain falls between her ample cleavage.

"Deputy Kyle, I have spent the last eleven years trying to push that man out of my mind other than what I have to endure until my boys reach adulthood. I don't make it my business to know if he makes enemies. But if that man raped a scared eighteen-year-old on her prom night, maybe the Minnesota police should sniff around about him doing it to other women. They may know more. Women up there may have boyfriends or husbands who don't like him. Who knows? All I know is that he hasn't contacted me in a few months, and I don't give one good God damn shit. Oddly, my boys haven't been fucked with it either. They asked about it a couple months ago, and I told them their dad hasn't contacted me. Am I free to go?"

I lean back in my chair when I'm done typing. Her eyes flick to my belt buckle, and I swear that her eyes darken before quickly bouncing to the floor. Is it possible this woman thinks I'm as attractive as I think she is? I mean, I'm in the prime of my life. At thirty, I have a full head of dark curls that I keep short and tamed, stubble the ladies usually like, and dark eyes to match. I lift weights regularly, and some of the older guys make me do the running down of perps when we're in a foot chase because they can't. Cheryl's beautiful, but she's not completely out of my league.

Hey, if my boss, who is an elected official, can marry a stripper next week, I can ask one out.

Before I can open my mouth, she stands. "I'll take that as a yes. I have to get to work."

"At Lucy's pole gym or at the club?" I ask as she turns to walk out of the bullpen. I also stand out of respect for a woman since my mother taught me right.

She looks at me over her shoulder, and that red hair I'd like to wind around my cock slips over her shoulder. "The club, Deputy Kyle. I still have to feed my boys, and tips mean food. Maybe I'll see you there again sometime."

Brat. I can't let her have the last word, especially not when she's addressed the elephant in the room that she recognizes me as someone who watches her dance from afar.

I clear my throat. "We'll let you know when we find him," I say.

"Oh, I'm on the edge of my seat."

She walks out of the bullpen, and the door swings shut behind her. Through the windows that separate the hall from the bullpen, I watch her walk toward the station entrance, her hips swaying so gracefully that I long to put my hands on them to feel the movement. It would be like dancing behind her. Only a professional dancer can move like that. Like she's waltzing as she walks.

Maybe she'd be a ballerina in another life. Not in this life, though. In this life, she was railroaded from whatever wonderful life she could have had by a rapist who got to handpick the mother of his children.

She's also a woman who sees all that's wrong with society. She sees how those who would do people harm walk free while the ones who call their bluff and actually do something about needless harm to innocents are imprisoned and vilified. She sees.

But does she also see the darkness the way I can?

Something stirs in me, waking up like a lion. It's a sense of protection I haven't felt in a long time, not since I wanted to rage about a fourteen-year-old kid who was hurting from the worst life had to offer.

This woman.

I like this woman, and nothing bad will happen to her if I can help it.

Chapter 3

Cheryl

"Please. Stop."

The words come out of his mouth in a garbled sound like he has marbles stuffed down his throat. It's funny to watch him try to talk with stiff lips while his tongue slowly turns to stone. He flails lightly against the carpet under him as his fingers twitch.

I look around at the trailer where this piece of shit lives. An old couch sits in the corner, and I can smell it from here. He must sleep on it and not wash the cushions. It smells like sebum and a lingering musky smell I can't place. Beer cans are overturned on the floor. Empty containers from the fried chicken place a couple blocks away litter the coffee table, and I can't see the kitchen countertops for the dirty dishes. Even as I glance over at the refrigerator, I spot a roach inching its way up the old model from the early nineties.

"No. I don't think I will stop," I taunt, squatting down to see him better and instantly cringing at his dirty brown hair and pit-stained white T-shirt. My thighs scream at the squat, but I refuse to sit anywhere in his house. No way is my ass touching anything in here. Not to mention I'd leave fibers behind. Lucy was clear the night she helped me burn Daniel's body at a campground I'd never been to. She said that if this happens again, don't touch *anything*.

"Sounds like you want me to stop now. Funny how *you* never stopped when you should have. Did you, Troy?"

Troy Acox. Fucker.

Literally.

He came through the club three weeks ago, bragging about how he drugged his elderly neighbor and took advantage of her for years before allowing his friends to also pay for the honor. He came in with a bachelor party, so this revelation was several beers in. What he didn't brag to his friends about was that the poor old woman took her own life six months ago. Apparently, she'd gone to the doctor and had a sexually transmitted disease. Considering she hadn't had a boyfriend or husband in years, flags were raised. She figured it out, hanging herself and leaving a note to her sister about the shame of it all. Unfortunately, she didn't name names, so Troy got away with it.

Until he opened his mouth in a strip club.

I've spent the last few weeks looking around this town, sniffing everywhere I could, to find a man worthy of what I'm now calling "The Daniel Martin Treatment."

It's been calling for me since I got rid of Daniel. There's been an itch, more like a want, that I remove another cancer from the world. The event with Daniel was so inspiring and cleansing that I rode the high for weeks until the police called me in to ask if I'd seen him. Kyle Mitchell was a bucket of cold water in the face in more ways than one. First, it's obvious they're sniffing around. Second, Kyle Mitchell is a cool drink of water all by himself. He was on my mind for over a week after that meeting, especially the way his eyes moved up my legs. I almost spread them for him right there in the office so he could get a good look up my skirt like on *Basic Instinct*. But would a fine officer like Deputy Mitchell even be interested in such things? He's probably super uptight, and there's no way a man like him could be interested.

Either way, the yearning to kill another shit stain hit me in the face like a plank after that. I now understand all the serial killer films that talk about it being a compulsion. Even the air I breathe feels dirtier with the sheer knowledge that men who don't deserve to breathe the same air still exist in the same world as my sons. This has to be done so I can breathe again and so my boys can grow up without seeing these men get away with treating women like shit.

I roll my neck as the feeling I got standing over Daniel months ago moves through my body now. My fingers flex. The air in my lungs feels cleaner already, even standing in this filthy dump. I take gulping breaths and swear I can feel it move through my lungs and even down to my toes. My heart pounds like it does when you see a really cute guy...

Or one that deserves everything he's about to get.

I quickly shove the syringe of succinylcholine I got from a male nurse weeks ago into my pocket. Jonah broke his arm at school, and a quick ER visit resulted in me kissing a male nurse in the supply closet before asking a favor. I hadn't used the supply until today, and I don't know if the nurse will ever put it together why I needed it. I doubt he'll risk his career to point a finger at me over a dirtbag if it even gets that far in the news cycle or search. Either way, I now have enough succinylcholine to make sure half the dickheads in the county are temporarily paralyzed whenever I need it. My only concern was buying a box of syringes and someone tracing it back to me. Then again, the pharmacy guy probably just thought I knew a diabetic.

From there, it was easy enough to tell Troy I do private dances at clients' houses. I flick my eyes around the room and grunt. You'd think he'd clean up the place if he thought I was coming over to fuck him.

"Why?" he whispers below me. His lips don't work well, hence the one-syllable words. He breathes in short, rasping sounds, either from the injection or panic.

"You want to chat? OK. Let's discuss. How do I feel right now? Is that what you want to know?" I ask, taunting. "I know you're so worried about my feelings. Such a charitable and empathetic lad."

He gives a short nod. "Who?"

"Ah!" I wag my finger at him and cluck. "No, no, Troy. See, if you want to talk about feelings, we'll talk feelings. Not my name. Not why I feel the need to be the one who does this since you only know me as a stripper who danced for you and your disgusting friends."

I widen my stance. I wore a miniskirt, limiting the clothing fibers and hair I could possibly lose. Sure, that sounds dumb now, but I'm following the Lucy rule. No prints. No fibers that stick out. No footprints. Clean up well. That's how she told me she handled Murphy Beckett. With my thighs spread wide in a squat position, Troy can easily see up my skirt to my tiny panties with strawberries on them.

That's men for you. They could literally be staring death in the face, and they'd still take the upskirt shot opportunity.

"I'm feeling…" I trail off and purse my lips. I feign thinking by looking at the ceiling. "Free, Troy. I feel free. See, my ex was a lot like you. You can keep a secret, right? Well, his name was Daniel, and I killed him. It felt so fucking good to rid the world of that trash, so I'm going to kill you now because I bet it would feel even better to kill you. I've always wanted to do my part to make the world a better place. I just never found it until now. This is my contribution. Some people volunteer at food pantries. That never interested me."

His eyes move around the room like he's looking for something. An asset? A weapon?

"I'm sure you're wondering why, though." I hold up my finger like I just had a brilliant idea. The movement startles him and he flinches. "You're both men who thought you could take whatever you want when you want it. You think you can do things to anyone you want, no matter if that woman was a woman you met at a strip club," I say, waving my hand toward my chest. Troy's eyes follow my hand. "Or if the woman was an elderly woman who couldn't defend herself. You're in control, right? Our bodies should be submissive and giving to you. All of that?"

He scowls but doesn't speak. His tongue may be fully stiff by now. A slight whining sound comes from his throat, and I sneer at it.

"Your neighbor was a good woman, and you ruined everything about her." I wave down the length of his body. "She worked doubles at a diner, raising her kids on that money alone. She fostered senior dogs for the local animal shelter. Yet you were cruel to her, Troy." I hold four fingers up. "You let four of your friends be cruel to her, too. Those are the ones I could figure out. Now, I don't want you to worry about your friends. They'll meet justice someday, whether it's at the hands of a pissed-off stripper with a taste for justice or a jail cell." I lean closer to his face so that I'm hovering over him and let one long line of spit fall from my mouth. He doesn't move, can't move, as it dribbles from my lips and lands on his face. I smile and hide the sudden panic when I realize I just left behind DNA. Shit. Maybe the police won't run DNA checks all over his face. I wipe it away with a nearby piece of fabric he had on his coffee table and immediately shove it into my backpack. I'll ditch that, too.

"Not much you can do to warn your friends now." I shake my head and clear my throat. "Tonight is all about justice for your neighbor, Troy. And she'll have it. She'll have justice, wherever she is, for every sick fucking thing you did to her. For every sick fucking thing you ever did to any woman that I just don't know about. For every fucked-up look you've probably given girls waiting for a school bus and for every tongue wag you've given women walking down the street. You're my bitch tonight, mother fucker, and I take my community service time very seriously."

His eyes dart around the room again, red and panicked. A single tear ekes out of his left eye.

"Oh, are you going to cry for me?" I taunt with a chuckle. I bite my lip and pull the piano wire I brought with me out of my backpack, holding it up so he can see how he's going to die. "That's it, Troy. Cry for me. Let me see those wet, sloppy tears run down your ugly ass face while I choke the life out of you. Such an ugly son of a bitch. Is that why you had to drug an old woman? Couldn't get a woman your age to look at you or give you the time of day because you're mid? Oh, how I wish you could beg for your life now. Beg like she probably did when she found out or if she ever came to while you had her drugged."

His eyes are wide with fear as I straddle him enough for leverage but hover so I won't leave fibers or sweat behind. When I'm in place, I quickly slide one end of the piano wire under his neck and bring it around to the front of his body before crisscrossing it at his Adam's apple.

Blood pulses in my ears. I roll my neck and welcome the euphoric feeling rushing up my spine and curling around my shoulders. Chills. Tingles. Whatever the world calls it. It's orgasmic as power over this absolute piece of shit moves through my body, raising goosebumps along the path. I breathe like I've been underwater for minutes and am just coming up for air.

Because that's what it felt like to kill Daniel a few weeks ago...coming up for air. Air that had been denied me for far too long. After Lucy and I drove home from the burn pit at her friend's campground, it felt like shackles were removed from my wrists, and the air felt cleaner. Air that I will not deny one single other woman if I can help it.

I pull the wire taught and watch Troy's eyes bug out until blood vessels burst a few seconds later. I watch his lips and cheeks tremble, and the air feels clean again.

CHAPTER 4

Kyle

I hate formal ties, and I hate Aaron Dwyer for making me wear one. Not really hate. I guess, when you're getting married and have to wear a tux, you want the people around you to look halfway decent or be just as miserable.

I sit on the groom's side of the aisle next to Bertie, Aaron's assistant, and her husband. A row ahead of me, Detective Coleson pulls at his own tie. He wears them daily, so he should be used to them, but he still looks miserable. His hair is just-fucked messy, which tells me he may have an interesting life I never considered. Tilting my head, I squint and think about him. I guess I never really have before. Thought of him, I mean. The only way I ever think about him is to ponder how I can fly under his radar since I aim for invisibility at work.

At the front of the church, Aaron pulls on his own collar, his bowtie probably rubbing him the wrong way. A wry grin settles on his face as he watches his young daughters walk down the aisle, the youngest dropping bright red rose petals in anticipation of Lucy's entrance.

I have a love-hate relationship with my boss. I hate him like anyone hates their boss. He annoys me when he asks questions he should already know the answers to. He's just as malleable as my boss in my last department, though. I give him good, hand-fed info and then back away into the shadows, letting the boss feel like a genius while I collect a paycheck and stay out of sight. He's a decent enough man, which includes hating injustice as much as I loathe it. I can't complain about his character, and he won't allow corruption or bribes. You can't ask for more in today's political climate.

Organ music replaces the soft classical tune, and the congregants stand as Lucy enters the room. Glancing to the bride's side of the aisle, I catch a wisp of fabric on the far side of the pew away from me, but I know that figure.

Full breasts.

Small waist.

Strong legs that aren't covered in fishnet stockings today, but I'd know them anywhere.

An elderly woman stands and blocks my view of her, and I pay little attention to Lucy as she walks in front of me. Yeah, Lucy's pretty in her white dress, and I'm sure Aaron drools as he watches her walk down the aisle, but I'm too preoccupied with craning my neck to see Cheryl Briggs.

Taking a small step out of the pew, not enough to be weird or look like I'm interrupting the ceremony, I lean forward just enough to get a good look. Two boys, obviously Cheryl's sons, flank her on both sides. They're identical. That is, they certainly look the same. I guess they could be fraternal, but it doesn't appear that way. Both of them have sandy brown hair, full cheeks, and their heads are bent as they peruse the programs in front of them, bored expressions lining their faces. They look like the picture of Daniel Martin we were given to run through our facial recognition systems. Before I can help myself, I clench my fists. What Daniel did to Cheryl was bad enough, but I can't imagine having to love a person who looks exactly like the person who raped you. Then again, she has twins, so there are two little Daniels she can't ever get away from. How does she manage it? How does she feed, clothe, and love those boys when they look exactly like someone who's hurt her over and over again?

Women are vastly superior creatures. If there was ever a doubt in my mind about Cheryl being an inherently good person, that's been erased by this woman's sheer existence and the love for her sons. No matter what happens, women usually get on with it, picking themselves up and doing what needs to be done for the best of everyone near them.

I pull my eyes away from her boys as the minister tells us to be seated, and I watch Cheryl smooth her dress over her perfect ass before daintily sitting in the pew. From my angle, I can just see the way she crosses her legs and how the muscles of her thigh bend with the movement. She wears bright red lipstick with a navy-blue dress, and her red hair is curled back from her face in large curls, giving the impression of a 1940s pinup.

"Mitchell!" Coleson whispers a foot from my face, and I startle.

"What?" I mouth silently.

"I'm not going to the reception. Will you take the card I have for Aaron and Lucy?"

"Why aren't you going?" I ask quietly, leaning forward, so close that I can smell Coleson's aftershave.

"My mother is sick. I was up all night." That explains the disheveled appearance. I guess he wasn't getting fucked sideways after all. "I wanted to be here, but I have to leave right after they kiss. Can you take it?" He holds out a white envelope with my boss's name scribbled on the front.

I take the envelope from him and stuff it into my suit jacket. I wasn't going to go to the reception either. I was hoping to be here for the church wedding, leave right after slapping Aaron on the back, and be on my sofa with a cold beer in an hour tops.

But Cheryl may be going to the reception.

I look back at her and stare straight into her eyes. Her unblinking eyes. Perhaps Coleson's whispers were louder than I thought. Whatever the reason she turned her head this way, we lock eyes and stare at each other.

Everything falls away. Aaron says something about loving Lucy in sickness and health up front. Aaron's daughter does something cute everyone laughs at. That is, everyone laughs except me and Cheryl Briggs. We just stare at each other like we're the only two people in the room and like her sons aren't there wondering why their mother is staring at a man in a simple black suit who didn't even shave this morning. We study each other like a ritual display of love isn't happening feet from us.

At some point in my normal courting of past women, I would tilt my head, smile, or even make a "come here" gesture. I do none of those things. I simply study her face, unable to move my eyes away from hers. Her shoulders heave slightly like she's having the same problem or like our eyes are stuck. She doesn't smile. She doesn't wink at me. She makes no move to acknowledge she even sees me. We simply watch each other as Lucy and Aaron say their vows. I swear to fucking God that the air between the pews crackles with something I can't name. It's like the charge in the air before lightning strikes. We don't stop staring until organ music starts again and Aaron and Lucy walk down the aisle, breaking the spell with Aaron's boutonniere a foot from my face as he passes.

It's simultaneously the creepiest and most erotic moment of my life, and I pat Coleson's envelope in my pocket. My beer and sofa can wait. Cheryl Briggs needs a dancing partner.

***

"Just to confirm, did you order the pasta con broccoli, chicken, or steak, sir?" the server asks, leaning down next to my ear.

"I ordered the steak," I answer, not paying attention to the man.

I can't find Cheryl, and part of me wonders if she didn't want to come to the reception with her kids in tow. Thankfully, I filled out the RSVP card with my menu choice two months ago. I guess it's good I came after all so the money wouldn't have been wasted. At least I'll get a steak out of the deal.

The waiter hovers behind me as he makes his way around the table, confirming the orders for the other guests seated at the table. The ten-top consists of a couple of coworkers, Aaron's newly-found half-brother from out of town, who is also a cop of some sort, and the man's new wife. Before Bertie can answer her menu choice, the empty seat next to mine is suddenly full...of her.

Her smell consumes me when the spicy perfume mixed with a hint of laundry detergent hits my nostrils. I watch as she lifts her water glass to her lips, drinks, and then sets it down again with a red stain across the rim.

"Anyone sitting here?" she asks.

I shake my head. There's only one empty seat at the table. I glance at the other nearby full tables. "Not that I've seen. It didn't have a place card. Must be an extra spot. Probably because I didn't bring a date."

"Thank fuck," she whispers. "I was put with the boys at the kids' table, and I don't want to hear dick and poop jokes all night."

"What if I tell you dick and poop jokes all night?" I ask, deadpan and unblinking.

"I'll get up and leave your ass, too."

"Kids' table?" I look around and soon spot another ten-top with a handful of kids and two adults who are both tipping back glasses of liquor at the same time, looking positively miserable.

"They're old enough to sit at a table and not make a huge scene. I need adult conversation."

"Do you not get that where you work?" I ask. Shit. Why did I say that? She knows I know where she works, and now she probably thinks I'm a misogynistic asshole or taunting her. "I didn't mean it that way."

She tilts her head and smirks. "What way is that?" she asks. "You know what I do for a living. You should also damn well know I don't do a lot of talking. If I do, it's because some seventy-year-old man can't get his dick up, so he pays for talk time to feel like I give a shit about his problems."

I look around at the other diners at our table. Bertie and her husband are talking to the minister, Aaron's half-brother and his wife are confirming their orders with the server, and another couple nearby must either be newly dating or newlyweds because their foreheads are stuck together like they've been glued. Not one person pays attention to Cheryl's comment.

"That is...very blunt."

"I don't dance around much, Kyle."

"You remember my name?"

She leans in, bats her eyes twice, and licks her bottom lip. "What can I say? I like men with a bit of curl in their hair and killer smiles." She faces forward again and straightens her silverware as the waiter makes his way to her. She quickly explains she's moved tables, and she ordered the pasta. When he's gone, she turns back to me. "You seem like a nice guy to sit with."

Now it's my turn to smirk. "Is that so? You think I'm nice?" Heat blooms in my chest. I very much want to be nice to *her*.

"Yes."

I lean forward and meet her gaze. She instinctively shrinks back like she should. "What if I'm not nice? What if I'm a dirty cop?"

She shrugs. "You're not. I'd know. I've met my fair share of dirty cops."

I lean back in my seat. Confidence. I need to act confident here. A woman like her will want to feel like she's with a strong man. Safety. I'm good at being a chameleon, showing people what I think they want to see. Something stirs in my chest with her, though. I want her to see the real me.

Eventually.

That doesn't mean I can't turn on the Kyle Mitchell customer service team tonight, though.

I lean back in my seat, giving her space again, but I rest my arm over the back of her chair. I'm only inches from the back of her dress, and I could stick my thumb out and trace it over her zipper. "Just out of curiosity, what makes you think I'm nice?"

"Are you asking me to tell you what I see when I look at you?"

I bite my lip. "Yes."

She holds her left hand up into a fist. "You were raised in a small town." She puts a finger up like she's counting. "Something about you says small-town kid. I can almost see you riding bikes up to an ice cream shop or swimming at a local swimming hole."

I nod. "One of one."

"You love your mother."

"Doesn't everyone?" I ask.

"Not even close."

I guess she doesn't talk to her mother.

"You have the look of a man who was taught to take care of himself," she continues. "Clean nails. Pressed suit like it's either brand new or you know your way around an iron or steamer. Your tie isn't a clip-on, so you have a good relationship with your father or a fatherly figure. Back to your mother, though. Your body is fit and has a healthy glow. That's important since a lot of men may be fit, but they're also wan or look like they aren't getting enough vitamins. The bulky guys usually eat nothing but chicken. You've been taught to eat right by someone, or you know the benefits of vitamins. There's also a nice smell about you."

"A nice smell about me?" I repeat, smiling and stifling a laugh.

"You'd be surprised how many men don't clean their asses."

"I certainly would. What else?"

Before she can speak, we're interrupted by several things at once. The speeches start just as our server places our salads in front of us and another member of the catering team places rolls on our small plates. Cheryl digs into her salad after Aaron's brother's wife passes us the ranch dressing, and we both listen politely to the best man, a friend of Aaron's from college, speak about how Aaron would talk about Lucy in college, even after the initial breakup. The best man is happy Aaron and Lucy found each other again when they needed each other.

The crowd politely claps, and our table joins in before Bertie starts a conversation about police procedures where Aaron's brother is from. Their conversation quickly turns to drug enforcement, something that's never interested me, and Aaron's brother's wife wears a bemused expression, quietly shaking her head at times.

Next to me, Cheryl spears the last cherry tomato on her plate. "What do you think of me?" she asks.

I wave off my salad plate as a server collects it and turn a bit so I'm facing her. "You want me to dissect you the way you did me?" I ask.

Where to start? There's so much I see about her, but I can't say some of it out loud. I glance at the other table guests.

"Yes. I'd like to know which of us sees the other more realistically. Incidentally, how'd I do nailing you?"

"Nailing me?" I raise an eyebrow.

"You know what I mean."

I take a deep breath. "You got all of them. My mother did an amazing job raising me. My father taught me to tie ties. I grew up playing soccer in a small town of about five thousand people, I take vitamins daily, and I certainly wash my ass. Is that what you want to hear? The boring stuff?"

Something changes in her eyes. They droop. Darken. Clear liquid fills them for a split second, so quickly that I blink and the water is gone. Did I imagine it?

"I like boring, Deputy Kyle. I haven't had enough boring in my life."

I crack my knuckles under the table. Shit. She wants boring. That's disappointing because, as small-town I may have once been, I'm anything but boring compared to most people.

I inhale through my nose and let it out through the small opening in my lips. "This is what I see about you. You're a good mom. You love those boys," I nod in the direction of the kids' table. "In fact, I think you'd do just about anything for them." She stiffens, and I smile. Yeah. I got her. "You're protective of those you love, even of those you like. You like..." My voice trails off and I tilt my head as I listen to the band Lucy hired. "Jazz. You like jazz."

"How do you know that?"

"Your toes have been tapping under the table for ten minutes, and they've stayed surprisingly on beat. You know these songs."

She reels back and raises her eyebrows. "Aren't you the observant detective?"

"I'm not done." I look around the table and make sure nobody is listening. Leaning forward, I gesture for her to come closer so that our foreheads practically touch. "You use a spicy vanilla body spray and an off-brand Tide laundry detergent from..." I tilt my head, thinking "Costco?"

"You're giving Hannibal Lecter vibes. You realize that's incredibly creepy, right?"

I sit back in my seat. I didn't mean to creep her out. I have no intention of scaring her. I have every intention of getting her into my bed at least once. More than that if I can play this right.

"Do you know what else my mother taught me?"

"Besides how to name a scent?"

I take my napkin off my lap and set it neatly under the rim of my plate. I stand, and Cheryl looks at me with big eyes like I'm going to walk away. Holding my hand out, I bend a little like I'm bowing. "She taught me how to dance with a woman. Would you like to see?" I jerk my chin where Aaron and Lucy are finishing their first dance and the band is now inviting the guests to join.

She doesn't blink or argue. There's no hesitation. Her eyes lock with mine like they did in the church, and she slides her warm palm into my hand. I take it and lead her to the dance floor where others are trickling as their salads are cleared and bread refreshed. It won't hurt to get a dance in while we're waiting for our meals. How much can I fuck up before the steak is served?

I spin her around and confidently grip her waist the way I was taught. My other hand takes hers, and I hold it away from me, not wanting to grind against her. I was told to have a stiff frame and not have "spaghetti arms" as my mother called them after watching an old movie from almost forty years ago. She briefly raises an eyebrow and smirks, but quickly hides it, shifting her face into a blasé expression and looking at something behind me.

"I've heard you're working at Lucy's place more," I say, turning her to avoid other prying ears of nearby dancers. I want her to focus on me. "Taking on more classes."

"Are you stalking me, Deputy?"

"No, ma'am. Just an observation I heard through the grapevine."

"Funny how the grapevine works. We usually only care about the information that benefits us."

"How do you think it would benefit me to know you're working at Lucy's club more often?"

"Are you flirting with me, Deputy?"

"Yes," I say in a husky voice. No use lying. "Is it working?"

Her face reddens. Even her ears are pink. "Why me? What's so interesting about a stripper, especially when it's a deputy doing the flirting?"

I spin her again and even dip her, her hair falling back and her cheeks flattening. "Professions don't matter, Ms. Briggs. When a man sees a beautiful woman, he takes an interest. I was just making conversation with a woman I want to take to dinner sometime."

She blinks twice as I right her and get back into position. One of the sides of her dress has slipped down over her shoulder, and I quickly fix it, brushing the tip of my finger over her shoulder in the process. She shivers at my touch.

"Would you like to have dinner with me?" she asks. I can't tell if she's asking for validation or asking me out.

"I'm getting the sense that you think it's a bad thing for us to eat in the same room."

She jerks her chin in the direction of our table. "We're about to eat in a couple of minutes. Doesn't that count?"

"No," I deadpan. I have no idea what's making me so bold. I usually let women lead. It's often easier, but I want to lead her, partly because I get the whiff that Cheryl has no idea how much she sets me on fire. "I want to eat with you in a room without Bertie from the office watching me and where all the focus isn't on my boss, for fuck's sake. Not to mention, Lucy's kind of your boss now. I want dinner when we're not around our respective bosses. I don't think that's too much to ask."

At the exact moment, a server deposits my steak and Cheryl's pasta dish at our places and walks away. I hold my arm up for Cheryl to spin under my arm, and she giggles. The sound of her laugh sends shockwaves straight to my dick. Why is this woman so under my skin? Sure, she's beautiful, but I feel a connection with her like I could tell her things.

Secret things I've never told anyone.

She feels safe for me. She's not perfect, but I don't want perfection. I want beautiful but raw. I want shadows lurking off to the side of the light. I need someone I can relate to, and I feel strong with her. Like I can be safe and make her safe, too. It almost feels like we're already a team, and I can't put my finger on why.

We hesitate for a moment, both of us silently agreeing we'll finish the song and then eat as we slowly turn and step toward the edge of the dance floor.

"If I go out with you, you understand my boys come first, right?"

"Are we getting married when we go out?"

She shakes her head. "No," she scoffs.

"Dinner ain't that deep. I want to feed you a meal and have good conversation. Maybe some pie afterward. Do you like pie?"

"Yes."

I wipe a stray piece of hair away from her face, and her eyes follow my hand. "I like pie, too. It's my favorite. I don't want to get married that night, but if we end up married on our second dinner date, I'll just say now that I know your boys will come first because you're a good mom."

She stares for a moment like she can't believe someone admitted that they understand she's a mom and has obligations that don't involve blowing me at my every whim. Hell, maybe she's never heard that before. Then again, she gives off a vibe that she doesn't date that often. Even when I've seen her dance at the club, I get the impression she does her job and goes home.

"Did you not think I'd answer that way? Either way, I want to go out with you. I wanted to ask you out at the police station."

"Why didn't you?" she asks.

"That would have been very unprofessional, and Dwyer would have been pissed if I hit on you and then you complained."

"What if I complain now?"

"You won't. If you do, I've asked you out at a social event in public. There's no power struggle here."

She smiles a half grin. It's practically evil. "You don't think I'll turn you down?"

I get closer to her so our noses are only an inch apart. I itch to plant a kiss on her forehead to show that she's under my care now, but I refrain. I'd only have to move a little and our lips would touch. Her eyes practically cross as they stare at my mouth. "Not after the way we stared at each other in that church, Ms. Briggs. I think you like me and are a little curious to have dinner with me, even if it's to prove I'm an arrogant piece of shit like all the others."

The song ends, but we still don't move. We stand in place, my hand still at her waist. I drop her hand, though, and I immediately miss the warmth of her palm. I make up for it by squeezing her waist. God, I'd love to move my hand lower and grip her hips, especially during...

"I'll go out with you, Deputy Kyle. Just one dinner. That's it. One meal."

"First, you're going to have to stop calling me Deputy Kyle." I take her hand again, this time leading her back to our dinners. "Second, you may really like me and want to go out more."

She slides into her seat, picks up her fork, and shakes her head a little while focusing on her plate. "Not possible. I'm just not that kind of girl to fall for a cop."

***

I place my keys in the little pot that sits on my entryway table. I made the pot in seventh-grade art class, and I give the whale a little tap on the head like I always do. Old habits die hard. I've been doing that tap on the whale head every day since middle school. Call it my own little OCD routine, reminding me of a time before my life went sideways. On the off chance I forget the taps, I've even been known to get out of bed in the middle of the night and come do it.

I loosen my tie and open my phone, scrolling quickly to Google and to the page that I haven't closed out of since I last searched for info on Cheryl Briggs. It's hard finding things on her since being a stripper isn't exactly a LinkedIn kind of profession. I only found the basics on her. I found her high school graduation announcement, a birth announcement for her twins, and an old police blotter for a pot possession charge that was buried in the sale pages of an old newspaper back when newspapers had police blotters. There's also a short blotter on an Ulta shoplifting incident. I have a hard time being worried about transgressions from back when there *were* newspaper police report sections.

I lean against the counter and scroll through the few things I've found and then do another search for her hometown and her last name, hoping to find something on her family. There's not much there except for some obituaries of people I'm fairly certain were Cheryl's grandparents and great-grandparents.

"Bupkis," I say as I quickly take my jacket off and fling it on my nearby bar stool. "Except for stupid pot charges and stealing a lipstick when she was fresh out of high school, she's clean as a whistle. Who cares about that shit?"

Walking to the refrigerator, I grab a beer and then hightail it straight to my couch. I toss my phone onto the coffee table, refusing to search any more about Cheryl until I can ask her myself, and I flip through Netflix. When I find a buddy-cop comedy, I pull a blanket over myself and reach into the end table to find the one thing that takes the edge off every time. It's the one thing that's been the only constant in my life to help me unwind after a long day since I was a teen.

Uncapping the inch-long razor blade, I unzip and pull down my pants until I find a patch of skin that I haven't used in a bit, and I whisper the blade across the area, hissing as a thin line of blood appears on my thigh. I let out a long sigh and sink into the pain...the pain that lets me concentrate only on it and brings relief and comfort more than the hurt that's clouded my life for over fifteen years.

Nothing else has ever compared when it comes to chasing away the darkness.

CHAPTER 5

Kyle

"What do we have?" Detective Coleson asks.

I hand him blue gloves and hold out a container of cream he immediately dabs under his nose. I'm getting better about the smell at a scene. Decay has always bothered me, but it's easier the more I do it.

"Did you call Dwyer?"

I shake my head. "I didn't see the point of waking him in the middle of the night so soon after his wedding. He hasn't even left for his honeymoon yet. He'll just come in and nod anyway before doing a press briefing. Not much he can do that you and forensics can't."

He nods at me and wipes his eyes. There are new bags there. He looks worse than he did at the wedding two days ago. The unsolved murders several months ago aged him, but now he looks like hammered dog shit. I don't know if he's ever recovered from not being able to solve the cases. The main suspect, Murphy Beckett, killed himself before he could be interrogated about the deaths. Now that Coleson's having family health problems, my heart actually goes out to the guy.

Kind of.

Something still itches at Coleson about the whole Beckett thing, though. It definitely reeked of bullshit, but I know when to keep my mouth shut. Aaron still maintains the mafia thug murderer was obviously Murphy Beckett, who killed himself over murderous guilt, and it all worked out for the greater good in the end. Sometimes I laugh over how wrong Aaron Dwyer is, and how someone smarter than Coleson got away with murder a few months ago.

"Who found him?" Coleson asks.

"Landlady. She's out front. She called it in."

"Were you first on scene?"

"Yes. It was me," I answer. Part of the job of deputy is that we're usually the first to arrive at a bad situation once it's called in.

"Touch anything?"

I let out a long sigh, trying not to make it obvious. Does Coleson think I'm an idiot? Wait. Yeah, he does since I've spent the last two years on this force letting him believe exactly that.

"No," I answer in a respectful tone. One of these days, I'll win a fucking Oscar for this shit.

"How long has he been here?" Coleson asks, squatting over the dead body of Troy Acox we found two hours ago when the landlady came by to collect the late rent and noticed a smell coming from the trailer.

"Four days. Maybe five," I say.

"Cause of death?"

"Strangulation with something thin."

The forensic worker on the scene, a woman just out of grad school I haven't been introduced to who looks all of about twenty-five but is probably older, walks over. She nods twice at something and takes another picture before finally looking at Coleson, almost like he's an afterthought. "Piano wire is my guess. I'll have to check for metal fragments, though. He was injected with something, too. I won't know for a couple of days."

"Who the fuck are you?" Coleson asks, finally realizing he doesn't know the forensics worker. One of the benefits of working in a small county is that we know everyone who works in emergency services and we're all incredibly bothered when personnel turns over.

"Avery Broderick," she says, holding out her hand for Coleson to shake, and I take mental stock of her long lashes, sculpted cheekbones, and a small scar on her chin you can barely see. A light brown mole the same color as her hair is on her left jaw.

Coleson takes her hand, pumps it once, and then drops it. Immediately after that, she pulls a lollipop from her pocket, unwraps it, and shoves it into her mouth. She waggles her eyebrows at me instead of a proper greeting and then turns to the victim again. "I'd say that time of death is about late Thursday night.

Maybe early Friday morning, but I'll have to have lab time to do some tests on potassium levels. A neighbor says she saw him on Thursday morning, but he didn't show up to work on Friday morning. I'd say a solid Thursday night, as indicated by the fly larvae."

I turn my head, stifling a gag. That's the part that gets me about crime scenes. It's not the blood or the shape of the body. That's just part of death and murder. I'm used to the smell, or at least getting better at it. It's the insects that get me every time.

Avery talks about fly larvae like a champion and takes a long slurp on her lollipop before giving it a short, childish lick. She then sticks it right back into her mouth.

"When were you hired?" Coleson asks.

"Don't give her a hard time," I whisper. "She's just doing her job."

Coleson looks at me like he's never seen me before. Maybe he hasn't regarding talking back. I don't normally do it since I spend a lot of time trying to blend into the wall, but Avery Broderick is new at work and doesn't deserve shit. It's also important that I make friends with her as soon as possible.

"Dwyer hired me a month ago," she answers. "I just got out of academy training and finished my advanced degree in forensic science. I'm replacing Foster."

"What happened to Foster?" I ask, my brow wrinkling in concern. A lot got past him. He also led a team of incompetent fuck hats.

"Word on the street is he was incompetent as fuck," Avery says like she just read my mind. Hopefully, she really can't. "He could retire, so Dwyer encouraged it." She spreads her hands wide and does a jazz hands movement. "So here I am, mother fuckers. Learn to love me. I like my coffee black, I won't join your shitty bowling league, I won't tolerate any locker room talk about my amazing titties, and I like my donuts with pink icing and sprinkles when you put in the order."

A small smile lifts Coleson's mouth, and I can't help but stifle my own grin. Yeah, she'll fit in just fine.

"What else can you tell us?" Coleson asks in a serious voice, obviously now impressed with Ms. Broderick. Ironically, he probably doesn't care about her credentials, but Avery telling him to stick his bowling league up his ass is all he needs to fall in coworker love. Working for the police is a lot like prison. You have to stick up for yourself on your first day, or you'll be pounded one way or another. Avery Broderick just made it clear she's not anyone's little bitch.

"No fibers picked up that we can make out. We'll get the stiff out of here and vacuum before we analyze the bag and save everything for possible matches later if you ever find your own ass or a possible suspect. I have some footprints, but they look like standard flat shoes."

"Flat shoes?" Coleson asks.

"No treads left to indicate brand. We'll work on it. But I'd say, judging by the size and no tread, we're looking for a female size eight or a male with feet small enough to match his dick and a penchant for ballet flats."

Coleson and I both open our mouths, but nothing comes out. We just stand there processing what she said.

She waves to the coffee table. "Perp either wore gloves or wiped down. We don't have any prints to go by. No evidence of forced entry. The door was either unlocked or the dumbass knew the killer and let them in. No blood except for around the victim's neck that I can see." She sighs. "I'll do all the sweeps for hair, trace DNA, and shit, but this looks like a clean forensic murder on my end unless you pin down motives and alibis with suspects I can match shit to."

"Any suspects?" Coleson asks.

"Isn't that your fucking job?" Avery asks, tightening her ponytail and then waving her lollipop like she's wagging a finger. "I do the science. You do the nosing around slash amateur sleuth thing where you sniff around for people who hated the guy."

Coleson coughs while I work on controlling my mouth and shoulders so it doesn't look like I'm laughing.

We all stand in silence, Avery staring down Coleson and me while we wait to see what insulting but awesome remark will come out of her mouth next.

"I, uh, just wanted to hear theories from a forensic specialist," Coleson says.

"Fine by me. I'll do both our jobs today." She points her lollipop at the victim. "If I had to guess, judging by the trash in his trailer and the half-dead pocket pussy I found under his couch cushion, I'd say this douche canoe wasn't popular with the ladies. Maybe a woman he assaulted at one point? Look here." She squats and points to Troy's neck. "It got the job done, but it was a bit loose. The way the marks are shallow tells me the piano wire wasn't all the way around him as far as it could go. That likely means female strength or a very weak male. Possibly younger if a male is involved. A fully grown man would have pulled tighter, and that would have made the marks deeper. This was done in hate, though. You don't choke a guy with piano wire unless there's some rage. Dude definitely pissed someone off." She slaps Coleson on the shoulder like guys slap each other on the back. "Good luck finding out who had beef with this dipshit."

Coleson and I both nod, and I can tell Coleson's impressed. It takes a special hardness about someone to work a crime scene in any capacity, and she has it. We may as well get used to her because she'll be around until I retire. I make a mental note to bribe her friendship with her aforementioned donuts. No use making an enemy of someone obviously brilliant with an attitude to match. I may need her on my side one day.

After she ambles off with some kind of device she aims at the walls to look for blood splatter that may have already been cleaned, Coleson turns his attention back to me. "You've been on this force for a couple of years now, right?"

I nod. "Yep."

"Do you think this is related to the deaths from months ago?"

I look down at the victim and his gray body. His tongue lolls out of his mouth, and even as I watch, a roach crawls out of the man's ear canal. "No, sir. I think this is something new."

The person who did this is new and terrifying, but something about it scratches my brain. I know my county and know the mind of a criminal. Something in my gut says I've never seen this killer before. I look around the trailer and try to see it through a murderer's eyes.

When I glance down at Troy Acox, words come from my throat, words I suppress lest Coleson hear them. "Good for her."

CHAPTER 6

Cheryl

A knock at the door startles me, even though I'm expecting it. Jordan and Jonah hoot and holler like they're catcalling as I walk to the door. Turning, I point my index finger at them and screw my face into the stereotypical angry mother. Wide eyes. Flexed jaw. Both boys immediately knock it off and fling themselves onto the couch like I told them to do when we rehearsed how we treat Mom's dates.

"Remember, I actually like him. He's nice," I whisper. "Don't chase this one away. I think I already want a second with this one." I furrow my brow and something in my eyes softens my boys' faces.

Jordan looks at the floor. "Yeah, Mom. OK."

They're getting old enough to understand that Mom deserves happiness, and I let out a long breath, smiling before turning the knob. Kyle knocks again, but I still hesitate.

Taking the boys out of this, what if I screw this up? My life hasn't been simple the last few months with Daniel having his unfortunate accident, being questioned about his disappearance, having to work more, Lucy's wedding, running into Kyle at said wedding, and agreeing to go out with a man who could be the very one to throw me into jail if he finds out I'm the one who killed Troy Acox. I've tossed and turned the last three nights, wondering if I'm crazy for getting involved with a cop when I'm not exactly selling Girl Scout cookies around town. I'm doing my own brand of community service, though.

Still, dating a cop is stupid when you actively watch for men coming through the club who deserve a little extra karma. It's not like I can stop. I listen for them in every conversation now. I actively search for who is good and who is bad.

Is there a part of me that wants to be caught? That can't be it because I enjoy killing bad men. I breathed fresh and clean air after I killed Daniel. When that crisp breath went away, I killed Troy, and it came right back. I'm still riding that high, and I wonder if it will wane after the same amount of time again. Will I become a predictable, cyclical killer?

All I know is that Kyle Mitchell makes me feel safe, safer than I have since I was a child. That was before I realized my parents were imperfect, before men did me wrong, and before I became obsessed with the news and its never-ending stories of women being murdered by men. Is it because I see how Aaron protects Lucy, so I'm interested in the same kind of setup when it's a cop that has a name instead of a faceless badge number? Dancing with him last week felt like melting into someone. I could have held his hand all night. He's not the type I usually date since the guys I usually go out with are on the other side of the cell bars.

I swing the door open slowly to not appear too desperate, and I nearly swoon into the doorframe. Kyle holds out a bouquet of daisies with white petals and yellow centers. No man has brought me flowers since, well, ever. I reach for them with a trembling hand as I wave him into my small living room.

"I'll put these in some water," I say instead of a proper greeting. Shit. I'm doing this all wrong. I haven't even said hello.

Then again, he hasn't properly greeted me.

"I hope you're not allergic. I went with daisies because the lady said they were a good choice to show that I'd like to get to know you better."

Jordan snickers and covers it up with his hand. I glare at the back of his head. He must feel it because he slouches and covers his face.

"These are my sons. Jonah is the one with the combed hair. Jordan is the one who thinks daisies are funny."

"Hello," Kyle says with a friendly smile. Not like it matters. Neither boy looks at him. I chalk it up to them being kids and not knowing what to say. Thankfully, Kyle doesn't act hurt.

I walk into the kitchen, wondering what Kyle thinks of my tiny rental house. I'm only a few feet away, even when I'm standing in the kitchen and hunting for a jelly jar for the bouquet. My kitchen is functional and would never be Instagram influencer fodder, but it's clean with wiped countertops and a small table that barely fits four people around it. A small cart with my microwave and some snack food for the boys sits in the corner, and accordion doors leading to my yellowing washer and dryer from fifteen years ago are neatly closed. I hazard a glance into the living room and find Kyle asking the boys about the basketball cards haphazardly scattered across the coffee table. I thrifted the table from Goodwill when I moved in. It's scuffed but functional. So is the couch I bought off a family member of a neighbor who died about a year ago. Functional, that is. I hope the old woman who owned it previously didn't die on it, but it's a nice fabric and sturdy, so I don't really care. A small hallway juts off from the living room and leads to a bathroom with nothing but the basics, a small room containing bunk beds for the boys, and my room across the hall from theirs. I wring my hands a little because I bought the boys their bunk beds for cheap on Facebook Marketplace, but I haven't been able to afford my own proper bed. Will Kyle think I'm not a functional adult if we come back after the date and end up fucking on my floor mattress?

Just then, Lenore from across the street pushes the front door open and stops short when she finds Kyle sitting cross-legged in front of the boys. I walk into the room, and she gives me a silent smile. "I'll go out with him if you don't."

I laugh, and it feels good to cut the anxiety. "Lenore, this is Kyle. Kyle, this is my neighbor across the street. She watches the boys for me and thankfully takes payment in child drawings and macaroni necklaces."

Lenore giggles, and I once again thank the universe there's an old lady angel across the street who misses her own grandsons so desperately that she babysits mine for mostly free. I slip twenties into her mailbox when I get home from work, but I mostly make sure she has somewhere to go on holidays and someone to take care of her when she's sick. She says that's enough and even tries to give the twenties back to me, but I slip them under her door or hide them in places in her house so she'll think she hid them herself. She's in her late seventies, so I know she needs the money to supplement her social security. If I have an especially good night, I always hide big bills in her couch cushions. One of these days, she'll find them.

"Don't forget the hugs," she says, opening her arms.

That's too much for my boys, and they both bolt off the couch into her, practically knocking her over. They don't have their own grandmothers around except for seeing them two weeks out of the summer, and Jonah and Jordan both love Lenore. Jordan goes out of his way to ask old men at the grocery store if they need a wife. Nothing like a ten-year-old trying to set her up because he desperately wants her to be happy and not so lonely.

"Are you ready to go, Cheryl?" Kyle asks, handing a card back to one of the boys and standing. He runs his eyes down the length of my body, warming me as he goes. I'm wearing the same dress I wore to the wedding, hoping he doesn't notice. Do guys notice those things? Either way, it's all I have, but I paired it with some new-to-me hoop earrings from the antique shop. "You look beautiful."

I run my hands over the front of my dress. "Am I dressed OK? We're not going hiking or anything, right? I can change into pants." I jerk my thumb over my shoulder in the direction of my small bedroom behind the kitchen.

I start to turn, rethinking my dress, when he waves his hands in front of him. "I love that dress on you. It's perfect. I made reservations at Prasinkos tonight."

My mouth drops open. That's where the rich people in the county eat if it's not dinner at the country club. Their truffled potatoes are legend. The wine list is so long it's dizzying.

"Should I wear something nicer?"

"No. You're fine. I'm fine like this."

He holds out his arms and I check out his gray pants that fit just right and his white dress shirt rolled up to show his muscular forearms. Fuck, those gorgeous forearms will be the death of me. No tie graces his neck today, and he sticks his hands into his pockets like he doesn't have a care in the world what the hostess will think.

He holds the door open for me, and we walk to his car in the cool evening air, a sleek black Volvo sedan. "No cherries and berries tonight?" I ask. "I'm almost disappointed."

He runs a finger over the hood on his way to open the car door for me. Talk about chivalrous. "Not tonight. I busted the real car out for you."

I slide into the beige leather seat and notice the clean smell of the interior. There's only a hint of his cologne. He circles the car and slides into his own seat. "What kind of music do you like besides jazz?" he asks.

"I get to pick? I thought the old saying was that driver picks the music and shotgun shuts their hole. Something like that."

A stoic expression crosses his face. "I understand that reference."

I giggle like a schoolgirl, and the sound is practically foreign. It's been too long since a man made me laugh. He's gorgeous, has a decent job, is nice to my kids, has a clean car, *and* is a *Supernatural* fan? I should hold on to him with two hands.

We chat on the way to the restaurant. He asks me how my son broke his arm, probably noticing the cast at the house, and I ask him about any interesting cases at work. I pass it off as being interested in general county gossip, but I'm dying to know if he'll share anything about Troy. I know he was found because I've been watching the news. I know they have no suspects because that's what the news says. Is that the truth? I smile and run my hand up Kyle's arm, watching the goosebumps rise on his skin as he talks about no suspects and gives little information. They've asked people who knew Troy, because it's usually someone the victim knows, and it turns out that pretty much everyone who knew Troy Acox wanted him dead. I settle back and listen as Kyle talks about Dwyer and someone named Detective Coleson until we swing into the valet station at the restaurant.

Kyle gallantly helps me out of the car, and I let him walk me into the restaurant, not dropping his hand when he takes mine. There's something about holding this man's hand. I feel like a middle schooler who is holding a boy's hand for the first time. It's just fingers and his palm, but it makes me feel...special. Maybe it's the heat of him, but my heart pounds, and my pits sweat.

Once we're seated at a quiet booth away from the entrance and kitchen, Kyle finally drops my hand so we can look at the menu. "Favorite food?" he asks, his eyes moving up and down the menu.

"Steak. You?"

"Also steak, but I order lobster when it's available. Guess we're a surf n' turf couple, huh? That could work out well for us. Why didn't you get the steak at Dwyer's wedding?"

"Wow. Stalk much? You remember I got the pasta?"

"I'm a police officer, Cheryl. I'm always going to be a little more observant than the average guy."

Let's hope he's not *too* observant, or I'm in deep shit.

I take a sip of my water and immediately smile as a young man practically bounds to the table to take our order. New waiter. Obviously. Kyle orders the lobster, and I order the steak. A bottle of wine shows up at the table, and the sommelier has Kyle taste it. Only when Kyle approves it, does the man pour our wine and walk away.

I lean forward until the goal of Kyle's eyes flicking to my cleavage is achieved, and I drop my voice. "I like pasta con broccoli, but I can't ever get the sauce just right when I make it at home. I can cook the hell out of a steak, though. That's why I got the pasta at the wedding." I don't mention that I don't cook much steak or fancy pasta anyway since I'm too broke to afford either, but that's not the point.

We chat about mundane things until our food comes, and when the food finally arrives, Kyle offers me some of his lobster. I almost ask him to switch me once I dip the white meat in butter and let it roll over my tongue. Kyle grunts in approval and nods at the taste of my steak.

"Why did you decide to be a cop?" I ask between bites of food.

His eyes grow dark. "To help people. I think, on some level, that's why a lot of us go into it. Either that or a hero complex. I probably have a little of both. At least, those two reasons are why the good cops go into it. The bad go into it for other reasons."

I take a drink of wine. When I place the glass down, I ask, "Why do you think the bad cops go into it?"

"Power and retribution. Those are their two reasons."

"Can you explain that?"

"Power is that they want to be bullies, basically. Imagine the worst high school bully in a movie you've seen. If they become a cop, it's because they think they can hide behind a badge. I knew a guy in the academy back in New York who used to talk about how he couldn't wait to flip his badge out if he was ever in an argument or some kind of fight. Once I got to know him, I learned he was picked on in school for not being the brightest bulb. This was about revenge for him. He had a chip on his shoulder, and wanted the opportunity to prove himself. Turns out, departments saw right through it and never hired him. Last I heard, he was working at a restaurant as the bar manager. As far as retribution, some cops may hate a certain group of people. They go into it to legally be able to hassle those people."

"Are you from New York City?"

"State. I grew up in a small town outside Buffalo. When I first became a cop, I worked in Buffalo."

"Why'd you leave?" I ask.

He doesn't have kids or a spouse, so he didn't have to move over a custody dispute or job transfer. At least, I don't think he was ever married. Does he have an ex or something?

He looks at the wall behind me, and his eyes shadow. There's a sudden glaze to them like he's a million miles away. "I just needed a change of scenery. Something not too small but not attached to a big department. A county deputy just outside Chicago was perfect."

"Did you want to hide from something?" I ask with a chuckle.

Kyle laughs, but the smile doesn't reach his eyes. It shuts my chuckle down, and I grip the cloth napkin in my lap. I don't want to scare him away by being too nosy, but I also want to know as much as possible about Kyle Mitchell.

"I wouldn't say hide. I had my reasons to leave the area."

"Family issues?" Fuck, can't I shut the hell up? He obviously doesn't want to tell me.

"Nothing like that. I'm close to my family. Just some old shadows. High school shit. You know the kind." He shrugs and takes another bite of his lobster. "You just want to get away from the past sometimes and from people who knew you when you were a dumb kid. Sometimes, those are the people who see us during the worst times of our lives. It brings up memories of your rough time when you constantly see them. Does that make sense?"

"I get that."

"Good, because I heard myself saying that just now and thought it sounded crazy as fuck." He smiles again, and just like that, the shadows are gone.

I let out a sigh of relief and hide it with a smile. I don't know why I thought it was bigger than just a guy wanting to get away from his hometown area. I certainly understand that. I was given some looks after getting pregnant early. I was given some side eye when I told a few people it was from a date rape. I can't be the only person in the world who had something embarrassing or horrible happen to them and wanted a change of scenery. It's not like Kyle is a criminal. He's a cop, and I'm sure there are background checks and psychological screenings.

Heat moves to my face, and I quickly take a drink of water to hide it. I'm the worst person at this table. The man across from me is probably a damn saint.

"You OK?" Kyle asks. "You're red."

I fan my face. "Wine does this to me sometimes."

Kyle grins. "Want to go to a movie after this? We could also head into Chicago if you want to do something special."

I check my phone. "Actually, Jonah has a baseball game early tomorrow, so I'll probably need to call it a night after dinner."

His face falls, and I almost walk it back. Sure, I have to get up early to pack orange slices and get my kid to his baseball game, but Kyle seems sad I'm not spending more time with him. I eye the plate in front of me. Did he want me to put out for the nice meal?

Shit. I'm a stripper. He probably thinks I do that kind of stuff.

We eat in companionable silence except for some offerings to share and Kyle asking if I want dessert, especially that pie we talked about. I'm not sure who's paying yet, and I'm not sure if I can afford a slice. I mentally think about how many ones I have in my purse, and I can just about cover my own meal. Just as I'm done counting in my head, the waiter puts the check in front of Kyle, and he immediately picks it up, completely unbothered by whatever amount he sees inside the leather booklet. Kyle puts his credit card in the slot and sets it on the edge of the table.

He reaches over and places his hand on mine. Here it is. Here's where he says something like, "Why don't you blow me in the car on the way home for the steak." Here's where I hear, "Want to go to a hotel for a bit before I have to get you home?"

"Would you like to go out again sometime?" he asks. "Maybe a time when we can spend more time together? A weekend during the day?"

I almost do a double-take. Is it possible he wants to actually spend time with me like I was hoping? Does he actually like me for more than my tits? Some men just want to watch a redhead blow them, but Kyle actually wants to hang out with me.

"Um, weekend days work well."

"Maybe we can head down to Lakeshore and do something along the water there. Do you bike ride?"

Why the hell are my panties suddenly wet at the thought of riding bikes with Kyle? It's not exactly an activity that screams sex. But my head goes to a funny place as I imagine a sunny day with a slight breeze ruffling his curls as we ride around Lake Michigan, pick up a game of beach volleyball, or share an ice cream cone.

He's helping me out of my seat before I know what's happening. His hand is on my lower back, and it's warm. It feels like it belongs there.

I'm barely thirty and have never been treated so well. So cherished. Is this what it's like to be swept off your feet by a hot man? If only he wasn't a cop who could slap the cuffs on me at any moment for offing my shit ex and a rapist.

I mull this over as we ride home in silence. His hand is on my thigh, and I leave it, enjoying the feel of his splayed fingers as he covers as much of my leg as he can touch. If it were any other of my dates, he'd be pushing his fingers inside of me or squeezing my breasts at this point in the night. I'd let Kyle if he tried. Just for him. No batting him away or pressing myself up against the passenger door as far as I could get. For now, I'll enjoy getting to know him and taking his touch day by day, maybe a little more exploration every time we see each other.

When he pulls into the driveway, he opens the car door for me again and holds my hand on the way to the door. "Are the boys still up?" he asks.

"Probably. I'd ask you in, but it's complicated."

He presses his forehead against mine, and my legs nearly buckle at the sweetness of the gesture. "I didn't expect to come in tonight, Cheryl."

"Y-you d-didn't?" I stammer, surprised.

"No. I want to wait anyway. Get to know you. Is that OK?"

It's more than OK. The urge to skip up the street hits me like a punch to the chest, and I'm sure the smile on my face is absolutely ridiculous. Never, in a million years, did I think a guy like Kyle would want to get to know me.

Wait. Does he know I'm a killer and is just testing me? Did my prints already come back from Troy Acox's trailer? I hope there's not a team of police waiting in my shrubbery to jump out and yell, "Just kidding! You're under arrest. Hope you enjoyed your last steak."

"I've rushed into things before with women I really liked, and it didn't turn out that well," he says. He tilts my chin up with his index finger. "You're not just a fuck to me. I think you're someone I can enjoy talking to and could really connect with."

My smile must be answer enough. Before I can form words and scream that I'll be happy to marry him and bear his children, he tilts my chin up even more and places his warm lips against mine.

There's no urgency or rush to delve into my mouth. He simply places his lips on mine and waits for me to catch up, opening my mouth slightly so his tongue can explore. He tastes of wine and a hint of the butter he dipped his lobster into. The combination is rich and makes me want more. If he ghosts me, it will ruin lobster for me forever.

I deepen the kiss as I wrap my arms around his muscular back. My breasts crush against his chest, and the nipples peak, chafing against my bra and wanting more than they'll get tonight. He cups my cheeks and gently strokes my skin as he works his mouth over mine. My entire body suddenly aches for his.

I open my eyes just to see what he's doing, and I find his eyes still closed as he breathes through his nose like he's never going to stop kissing me. Maybe he won't. Maybe I don't really want him to ever stop. One of my hands roams to his hair, and I tease a spot of curls, pulling them through my fingers and enjoying the feel of them springing back into place.

When we finally break apart, he places one more soft kiss on my cheek. "Good night, Cheryl. I'll call you soon. Probably sooner than you think."

He walks away, and I fumble with the door. Once I get into the house and Kyle is driving away, I press a palm against the wall and bend over, catching my breath. I've never been kissed like that before. Never in my whole life. It was like I was important to him and, dare I say, loved.

My phone buzzes, and I fumble through my purse until I find it and Kyle's name on the screen. Sliding the button to answer it, I press it to my ear. "Didn't you just leave?"

"I told you I would call you sooner than you think. It's supposed to be nice this weekend. Want to go to the aquarium before taking a walk? The boys can come if you need to bring them."

Do I want to bring the boys on a second date? No, but it's sweet Kyle even considered them. That's never happened before.

Besides, they're old enough to be OK for a couple of hours in the afternoon, especially with Lenore across the street. I wouldn't leave them at night without someone trustworthy nearby, but they're at an age where they can manage if I feed them lunch before I go so they don't have to use the toaster or microwave.

"I'd love to, but just you and me for now, Kyle."

CHAPTER 7

Kyle

"Kyle, what the hell are you doing?" Aaron Dwyer's voice asks through my personal walkie that's connected to one inside his car. He has several radios in his vehicle, one for five deputies. One is, unfortunately, connected to its mate in my car.

I pick up my device and hold it to my mouth. "Just keeping an eye on things. Over."

"Why?" he asks again.

I blow out a breath and pinch the bridge of my nose. I hesitate before hitting the button again so I can find my words carefully. "I just have a feeling that I need to watch here for a bit."

To say I've had lots of feelings at work and in my personal life since Cheryl Briggs walked into my world is an understatement. I've spent a lot of time trying to get a read on her and some things at work that are just...off.

"Do you have to have a feeling in a strip club parking lot?" Dwyer asks. "You're in your work vehicle. If someone sees it in the lot, they may think our finest are in there getting dances on taxpayer time."

I roll my eyes. He's one to talk, but I won't go there. "I'm clearly inside the vehicle. My window is rolled down. My forearm is out. They'll know I'm just sitting in the lot, sir." Fuck, I hate that he can track my vehicle.

"Do not let me catch your ass in there, and find something else to do sooner rather than later."

"Yes, sir."

I place the handheld, long-range radio back on its stand and grit my teeth. I won't let him catch me, at least. But something is up. Troy Acox visited this club, and I know it because Coleson asked a few of his friends when the last time they saw him was. It was uncanny that it happened to be the place my girlfriend works. I just can't tell if my intuition is firing on all cylinders because the club is somehow connected to Troy Acox's murder or if I just hope the club is involved because I want to spend time watching where Cheryl works a couple times a week.

Today happens to be one of her days on shift, and it's around the time she usually takes a break.

I glance around the parking lot and spot the cameras Peter, the owner, has up to monitor the girls as they walk to their cars at the end of their shifts. From experience, I know that the bouncers also stand outside the door until the girls get into their vehicles, but part of why I'm here is to make sure she's safe if she steps out on break. Call me protective, possessive, creepy, or any number of adjectives, but I know she's in there. I know she's being groped by men and having dollars thrown at her. Do I trust her? Yes. Are we exclusive? We haven't talked about it, but I'm certainly not seeing anyone else.

My cock strains against my pants, and I look behind me. I parked near the dumpster at the back of the lot. I can see the door, but I don't think anyone at the door could see me unless they strained their necks to the right. There are no cars parked next to me. The club isn't busy since it's daytime. The cameras that monitor the lot won't pick up anything happening in my car.

I unbuckle my pants and slide my hand inside my boxer briefs. I have half a chub, but it soon moves to full mast when I spot Cheryl walking out the side door that leads to the dressing room. I can barely see her, but the red hair sticks out. She takes deep breaths like she's on a break and the club is stuffy. She rolls her neck and pulls out her phone, scrolling while I watch her. I grin, hoping she's texting me or scrolling my Instagram page. She unwraps a small energy bar that she hid in her hand that I didn't see. Snack time, I guess.

Great, now I'm thinking about her mouth and the idea of my salty taste rolling over her tongue instead of the energy bar. Fuck, she's beautiful. My cock twitches in my hand, and I jerk it softly as I admire her fishnet stockings with strategic tearing up the seam. From this distance, I can't see the detail on her bikini top, but something glistens. Sequins? She's in her street shoes since she's on a break, but her legs still look long and lean. From there, it's easy to imagine them wrapped around my waist as I pump into her.

"Fuck," I whisper, speeding up my rhythm and rubbing the head of my cock every time I pull. My balls tighten, and I work myself, thinking about how good her mouth would feel and about how much I want to bury myself inside her warmth. I whisper her name, and I know how creepy this is, watching her while she's on her work break.

I open my thighs wider and gasp as cool air hits my engorged balls. Looking down, my dick is an angry shade of red as I work the precum around my length and take slow pulls, whimpering a little each time I fist the head. Up. Down. Up. Down. I lean back against the headrest, but I don't dare take my eyes off her. There she is, scrolling her phone so innocently as I imagine how she'd say my name in bed, how she'd bend over for me, and how that silky red hair would feel wrapped around my fist.

I reach in with my other hand and cup my balls, using two hands to get myself off. Would she also play with my balls while she blew me or jerked me off? Something tells me she knows exactly what she's doing with pleasuring a man. Anticipation for her moves up my spine, and my balls quiver in my palm. I'm not sure if it's because I'm jerking off or because the idea of getting this woman in my bed is so exciting.

My balls stiffen in my hand. I know the drill and let go, quickly grabbing a nearby tissue I keep in the car for crying crime victims. At the last millisecond, I use the tissue to catch white, hot cum from my trembling body.

"Fuck, Cheryl," I whisper as the last drops drip onto the sopping tissue.

She's still standing against the wall and chewing the last bites of the energy bar, completely oblivious that I'm watching her or even that I just enjoyed myself while watching her.

I leave my pants undone. Leaning over my console, I open the glove compartment and pull out the pocket knife my father gave me when I joined Cub Scouts twenty-four years ago and a small lighter that's almost out of butane. The knife fits in the palm of my hand, and I only use it on one occasion these days. Without this use, I'd have no use for a kid's pocketknife.

I grab a fresh tissue, flick the lighter over the tip of the knife, letting the flame heat it since there's no use getting an infection, and trace the edge of the blade just above where my trimmed pubic hair meets my thighs, careful to avoid major arteries or veins.

I let out a long sigh. God damn, the blade is better than a fucking cigarette after one hell of an orgasm.

CHAPTER 8

Cheryl

Sweat glistens on Jake Portsmith's bald head, and drops dribble all the way down his face, finally falling to the ground after they converge at his chin. The front of his shirt is wet. Stains cover each armpit.

Geez, this man acts like he's halfway paralyzed and sitting in a firepit or something.

The need came faster this time. It was like an itch in my chest. I want it more often now. Even with my mind distracted by Kyle and how I'm going to buy gifts for my boys' upcoming birthday, I still spent way too much time thinking about killing Jake.

He was easy enough to pick up. I had to be careful, but I heard through the grapevine that he likes picking up hookers down near Main and Fourth Street on Thursday night. The grapevine being the back room at the club when my friend, Coral, said she just danced for a shithead who actually bragged about picking up street whores, fucking them, and beating them up so he doesn't have to pay.

It took a little detective work on my part, but I soon pieced it together that two women who had been found dead in the last five years were street girls and were picked up in that area. Nobody really missed them since they didn't have families or husbands. Only a cousin of one of the girls and a foster mother of the other raised alarms that their acquaintances were missing after weeks of no contact. It wasn't hard to figure out that Jake Portsmith obviously got a little too rough with both of them.

So I waited. I parked in the alley that meets Fourth Street, wore a tight little skirt, and kept my work heels on to look the part. Then I made my move, seducing him to get into my car as a change of pace.

It had to be my car because it's easier to clear the fingerprints and vacuum afterward to get rid of the evidence instead of worrying about wiping down *and* ditching his vehicle while ensuring no trace of me is in there. If they found his vehicle, they'd run prints, and I'm in the system after that pot bust so long ago. However, they would need to have a reason to search *my* car. Except for some homeless people that didn't pay any attention to me or Jake, the corner was very quiet, and the dumbass got into my car on the promise that I knew a perfect spot for giving him head for only a cool twenty bucks.

I lean over him and cock my head like I'm doing a high school chem lab and am curious about the results. I hum a little and cluck, not at all impressed at what I'm seeing. "Now, you may ask yourself, 'Why am I sitting in the middle of a firepit on a lovely evening such as this?' I assure you there's a very good reason you're here, Mr. Portsmith."

"What do you want?" he yells as loud as he can with his tongue just coming out of paralysis, the sound echoing across the campground. I cringe a little but don't let him see anything but the forced smile. Lucy told me that Ellen, whoever the fuck that is, doesn't rent out spots on this side of the campground. Still, there are people about a half mile away and across the creek. I can't get too loud. "Let me go. Did Leroy send you?"

I step back a bit and smile. "Who's Leroy?" I steeple my fingers under my chin. "I smell gossip. Spill the tea."

He shakes his head, whining a little and struggling against his zip ties I lifted off Aaron Dwyer's belt when he took it off to help apply painter's tape in the bathroom at Lucy's gym during his lunch hour. He responsibly locked it in the filing cabinet first, but I have a key. I only took two. I didn't want to take more in case Dwyer needs them. I only took one for Jake Portsmith's feet and one for his hands.

The succinylcholine I injected into his groin when I pulled his pants down to blow him is wearing off. I didn't blow him, and I laughed at the look of shock on his face as we wrestled with the empty syringe before the medicine kicked in. It's not every day that a guy expects a blowie but gets jabbed with a needle two inches away from his cock. Thankfully, it works fast, but it also doesn't last as long as I thought it would. It took some time to get him into the zip ties, drive to the campground, find the fire pit furthest from civilization, and drag him to it. When I finally got him sitting upright in the center of three small piles of kindling, his hands were already wriggling against the zip ties and his mouth called me every name in the book.

Honestly, I'm not sure how the guy from *Dexter* does all the setting up, murdering, cleanup, and dumping so quickly. I guess that's just Hollywood magic.

Better make this fast.

"I guess you're into more shit than killing women, huh?" I ask. "What is it? Money laundering? Gambling debts?"

He furrows his brow. "I've never killed anyone, bitch!"

I smile and then rear back before hocking a wet loogie right into the liar's face. Huh. Daniel used to do that to me, and other men have done it to me at the club, but it *really* feels like you're humiliating the other person. It feels good to do it to someone who actually deserves it. Powerful, really. I see the shame in Jake Portsmith's eyes as my saliva mixes with his sweat and works its way down his face.

"Don't lie to me." I pull out the yearbook pictures of the women he killed, women barely out of their teens, and throw them at him. They flutter in the air and look like Hollywood headshots since they're blown up to ten times the yearbook size. "Look familiar?"

He shakes his head, but there's something on his face and in his eyes.

Defeat.

"I didn't do nothing."

I squint. "Not to sound too much like my eighth-grade English teacher, but that's a double negative. Are you saying you *did* do something to them?"

He looks around, frantically looking for an escape route or help. Something.

"What?" he asks through gritted teeth.

I walk a few feet to my car, lift the trunk, and get the gas can. I can't take the chance that my fire-starting skills will be rusty or the wood will be wet.

"No! No! No!" he complains as I tip the gas can and let the liquid flow onto his head and down his chest and back. He closes his eyes and mouth, but he still spits some out as I move the can so that I saturate his legs and feet.

When the last drop of gas is on his body or clothing, I set the gas can down and sit on a big stone that's around the firepit. I smile at the thought of people sitting exactly where I'm sitting now and roasting marshmallows over an innocent fire while singing campfire songs. Maybe some graham crackers were involved.

Not tonight.

"Can I get your advice on something?" I ask. Jake nods slowly like he's willing to do anything to stay alive. "Is it hard getting rid of the bodies after you dump the women?"

He stares at me, unable to speak. I'm not sure if he's just worried about getting a mouthful of the gas still seeping down his face or if he knows he's caught.

I take out a book of matches and strike one.

"OK! OK!" he says, his eyes wide. "I fucked up. Is that what you want to hear?"

"Not really," I say. "I mean, it's good that we're talking this through and you're finally admitting to hurting women, but I'm sad for them. What was their big sin, Jake? Being a hooker? Or simply being a woman?"

"Both," he spits. His bottom lip trembles.

I tilt my head again. "Did Mommy not love you very much?"

He looks at me, probably running through all the answers he should give, trying to decide which one will get him out of this mess.

"How did you kill them?" I ask, shaking off the original match and impressed it took so long to burn down and twinge my fingers. The second match doesn't burn as long. I light a third while he thinks, but I throw this one near his boot. His foot twitches in response, but he still can't pull his foot fully away from the little matchstick. It doesn't catch.

"I s-strangled th-them," he eventually stammers through more lip trembling.

"That wasn't very nice of you. Why did you do that?"

He flexes his jaw. He's had enough of my shit. "Nobody would miss them."

"Tell me the entire reason."

"That is the entire reason!" he yells.

I lean forward. "It was also because they were pretty, and pretty girls don't look at Jake Portsmith. You killed them because you can't get a woman to suck your dick for you, and it makes you have big feelings. You thought you could get away with it, didn't you? You thought, because they didn't have families, that you would never get caught."

"They were trash anyway. I paid them to fuck me, and they did. Bent right over for it. I strangled them while I fucked them."

"Ah. I bet it's amazing to feel a woman stiffen and grow cold while you're still rawdogging it hard, huh?"

"Fuck you. I don't know why you're taunting me, but I'm going to do the same to you when I get out of here."

I open my mouth in delightful surprise and clap my hands a bit. "Bold words from a guy sitting tied up in a fire pit and covered with gasoline, but I don't think intelligence is your strong suit. If you think that I'm going to get you to confess what you did to those women and then let you go, you're a regular fucking comedian, sir."

"You don't have it in you to kill me," he says. "Bitches usually don't."

Redness seeps up his neck. Since I didn't light him up immediately after dousing him in gas, I guess he thinks I'm weak. Where there was fear, there's now hope that he'll be able to overpower me in minutes while I keep him talking.

After all, I'm just a woman and we do love our chatting. According to Jake Portsmith, we also don't have the balls to remove boils like him from the gene pool.

Too bad for him, I've never had a lot of girlfriends, and I stopped caring about being nice when Daniel grabbed my hair in that parking lot.

"Sir, with all due respect, I was able to lure you out to the woods, paralyze you, and get you into a fire pit. Do you really think you're leaving this little stone circle here?" I tap the brick around the pit and make a circular motion with my finger.

That shuts him up. He grits his teeth and rolls his shoulders against the zip ties as much as he can. We stare at each other for a minute as I let him think about the consequences of his actions.

Finally, he's had enough, and he kicks out at me, which is laughable because he can't lift his foot more than an inch. "You fucking cunt."

"That's not nice, either. Manners, Mr. Portsmith!" I hiss.

"You bitches all deserve it. All of you. Only good for one thing."

"What about cooking and cleaning?" I ask with a lilting grin. "I mean, guys like you think we're only good for that."

"I can order a pizza. Pussy is the only thing you're good for."

"Why are you so emotional? You all say women can't be trusted because of our emotions. Funny. I've only seen men like you act like toddlers with your baby tantrums. Rape. Kill. Steal. Steal. Kill. Rape. That's all men like you have done throughout history. If women are naturally meant to be weaker and submissive to men like yourself, why do our institutions have to work so hard telling us we need to be submissive? I mean, that's a pretty intense marketing scheme you all have."

I take a deep breath, and there it is. The clean air I associate with one less asshole in the world whistles through my lungs. The adrenaline courses through my veins like cold fire, almost like when I got a saline IV while in the hospital once. Cold at first, followed by a nice, relaxed feeling. It's a high I know I'll chase for the rest of my life or until something convinces me to stop. My lips move into a smile, and I turn my face to the sky, letting the breeze ruffle my hair.

I get off the rock, stand over Jake Portsmith, and flip through three matches, laughing as he flinches as I toss each one at his feet, knowing damn well they won't catch because I didn't put much gas on his boots.

"Stop. No!" he yells.

"Did they say those things?"

His face crumples, confused. "What?"

"Did they say those things? Did they fight? Want you to stop?"

He opens his mouth to answer, but no sound comes out. It's fine. I'm not really interested in hearing what he has to say. I know the women probably fought for their lives as best they could. Begged. Pleaded. All for Jake Portsmith to kill them and dump them God knows where in the end. The women he didn't kill had to go home and look at their bruised faces in the mirror.

Never. Again.

I give a one-fingered wave like I'm flicking a switch. "Bye, mother fucker."

I light another match, throw it a little higher than the last one, and hope no campers a half mile away hear the screams as they fill the night sky or smell the melting skin of Jake Portsmith's smug fucking face.

CHAPTER 9

Cheryl

"How much?" I ask, gawking at the lady in front of me. "When did they go up?"

The woman behind the counter shrugs, a blasé look on her face only a federal worker would understand. Since when did stamps cost so much?

"I thought a book was eleven dollars?"

The woman shrugs again like it's her only method of communication. Opening my change purse, I paw through my coins. Tons of pennies. No quarters. Just my luck.

"I got it," a familiar voice says behind me. I turn slowly to find Kyle the second person in line and holding a tube package. "May I?" he asks the person in front of him, gesturing.

Maybe it's the fact that he's wearing his black cop uniform, but the person in front of him in line steps aside and lets Kyle jump the line. He's soon at the counter next to me.

"Fancy seeing you here," I say. "Were you following me?"

"Need some help?" he asks, reaching for his wallet.

Oddly, the federal worker behind the counter smiles for him. No shrugs. Well, he's hot, so I understand her change in attitude. He smiles back at the worker, and my stomach drops in an odd mixture of *that's mine* toward Kyle, and *hey, bitch, that's mine* toward the post office worker.

"I can get half," I say to the worker. "I just don't have extra cash on me and my bank doesn't have my check yet."

Peter doesn't pay us in direct deposit. I only get cash at the club or a monthly check with a bare minimum hourly rate, and I thought I brought enough cash. No one with half a brain would walk around with the stack of ones strippers get on an average night. Lucy pays me for teaching classes by direct deposit twice a month, but that's not until Friday. I can't let Kyle pay for me. He already bought me dinner. If I let him provide for me like this, he'll be no different than the men at the club, raising their dollar-filled fists in the air and waving them around.

"Cheryl, it's fine. If you're so fluffed about it, buy me a beer next time we hang out."

The postal worker's face falls like she just realized she doesn't have a chance with him. Tough shit, honey. The more I run into Kyle Mitchell, the more I want him to be mine. Believe me, that idea decimates me, given my hobbies. What the hell am I getting into?

We spent three hours in Chicago last weekend, and I hated telling him I had to get back to make sure the boys hadn't burned the house down. He dropped me off, gave me another kiss, one a little sexier than the kiss on our first date, and then left without making another date with me. He's texted me twice with very short conversations, but he hasn't asked me out. Does he not like me now? Does he think dating a woman with children isn't worth it? I hadn't heard from him in five days except for a few quick texts. I made myself busy with killing shitheads, but I was still hurt not to hear from him.

I accept his help now, letting Kyle swipe his debit card for the stamps, and I slide the eleven dollars in cash I have in my hand into his warm pants pocket. He enters his pin number into the machine and gives me a look that screams *you're trouble* out of the corner of his eye.

"Take it out," he mutters after he's done and the postal worker prints his receipt. He hands the stamp book to me.

"No," I say primly. "You just want my hand in your pants again."

"That's a perk, and we'll get to that someday if I have my way, but I don't need the cash right now."

My stomach flutters. That's not something a man says to a woman he's lost interest in.

"That and a beer, Deputy Kyle. That's what we agreed on."

He sighs, grabbing my elbow and moving me out of the line. He leads me over to the little desk where people can fill out custom forms.

"Why do you do that?" he asks, dropping my elbow.

My forehead crinkles, and I squint. "Do what?"

"Not allow someone to help you."

"I don't know what you're talking about, but I don't need charity."

"I didn't say you did," he says, brushing back a lock of my hair that's fallen out of my ponytail. "It's not charity. It's me enjoying helping the woman I like."

The woman he likes? OK, so it's official. Why do I feel like a teenager and the cute guy from math wants to dance with me at the school dance? Something about Kyle is so pure, so good, that I can't help but swell with pride that he likes a girl like me. Guys like him watch girls like me dance and admire our bodies, but they don't *like* us as human beings.

Then again, he knows nothing about my extra-curricular activities. That would turn him off.

"Let me help sometimes," he says, wrinkling his forehead. "I need that. It makes me feel special to you. OK?"

"It's hard for me to accept help."

He tilts his head and sticks the tube under his armpit. "Why?"

I let out a half laugh. "It's what I'm used to, and now I'm just comfortable with it. I gave birth alone. I rode home from the hospital with the boys in an Uber alone because my mother had a hair appointment and my father wouldn't take the day off work to help me with what he called 'my problems.' I taught myself how to change a diaper. I have parented alone, taught myself to cook basic things so the boys ate healthy enough, and signed up for everything an adult needs alone. Not one person showed me how to turn on water or electricity in my name. I went to get a bank account alone. I…" My voice trails off. I have no idea why I'm telling him about the last eleven years of my life, but it's like a chest wound has opened and is gushing out onto the post office floor. He watches me like he's a licensed therapist and paid to listen to me drone on about my issues. "I moved alone. I enrolled my kids in school alone, bought my car alone, fought Daniel in court alone, and did my best to get through every single fucking day of my life totally and completely by myself." I take a deep breath like I've been singing for a full minute without a break.

He's silent for a moment until he finally cups my cheek. I close my eyes and lean into the warmth of his palm. "You may have had to do those things by yourself in the past, but you don't need to anymore."

I smile again and shake my head, my eyes drifting to the floor. I still don't believe it's possible to have someone at my side to do things or help me. "We've had two dates, Kyle."

He steps closer to me and nudges me closer to the wall where the old woman who just finished at the counter won't run into us or even hear us as he whispers. He bends a little so our faces are even and holds my eye contact like I do when my boys need to understand something very important. "Cheryl, listen to me. We may have only gone out twice, but I feel like I've known you for more than two dates. We talked at Dwyer's wedding. I interviewed you about Daniel." My heart pounds remembering that, mostly because the entire conversation that day was a performance. "I've seen you dance at the club before that."

I wipe my nose. "I didn't think you'd like me after that. Most men lose interest or only want my body."

"I won't lie. You're fucking gorgeous. But I'm getting to know *you*. I want to take this further and continue seeing each other."

"But you haven't called since Chicago."

He lets out a long sigh. "Oh, you think I was blowing you off?"

I nod. "Yeah. I didn't call you because I didn't think you wanted to talk to me."

"No, sweetheart. Another deputy was hurt on duty. Dwyer has me out on his night patrol this week, and I've been sleeping most of the day. I haven't been able to call or go out. I don't know when they are going to pull me off nights, so I've been hesitant to schedule something. I'm off Saturday, but I know you work Saturday. Any time I'm awake and thought to call you or schedule something you're at work or at Lucy's gym. I could only text, and I'm not the best at conversation over the phone anyway."

"So you aren't blowing me off?" I ask.

He smiles. "Not even a little, and I hate that you thought that." He looks at his watch. "Let me mail this poster to my mother and then I'll take you out for ice cream or something. Do you have to get back to the boys?"

I pull out my phone and check the time. "They get off the bus in an hour."

"Perfect," he says, already heading to the line to ship his package. "Just enough time for frozen yogurt."

Chapter 10

Kyle

I have no idea why I'm here. Coleson called and said he needed me to help go through the victim's things, but I'd rather get a bout of syphilis than go through this loser's belongings. That's clear the minute I roll up to Jake Portsmith's rental house.

A hiker called the death in two days ago. Since then, Coleson's been in a tizzy. He now has a guy killed by piano wire and a guy burned to death. Granted, there wasn't much left of Jake Portsmith, but Coleson thinks the killer got spooked and heard someone. Maybe Portsmith screamed too loud. Whatever the reason the victim was left in the pit, there was still some of him visible when the responding officer on shift showed up. Apparently, fat and muscle melt in fire, but some of Portsmith's skeletal remains were simply charred. We're dealing with a killer who thought the body would burn down entirely and didn't know they'd need a backup plan for the rest of the remains.

Amateur killer. Every professional psycho knows you need a backup plan to the backup plan.

Coleson wanted to drag the nearby pond to see if other victims had been disposed of after being burned. Dwyer merely squinted and denied the request for dive equipment and team, muttering something about the killer obviously not knowing they'd need to dump what wouldn't burn, and he isn't going to spend taxpayer money unnecessarily dragging a pond.

Interesting. Usually, he's a thorough man. I would have dragged it, but I watched him shake his head and train his face into a neutral expression when he told Coleson we aren't going to mess with it. I know his tells, though, and I watched his eye twitch for a few seconds. He inhaled deeply through his nose, which is a sign of annoyance to a man as calm as Dwyer. He was bothered by the request.

Either way, I'm on the case and Coleson's bitch for the day.

I trudge up Jake Portsmith's crumbling concrete porch and open the squeaky door with the screen hanging off the aluminum frame. "Coleson?" I ask, coming into the house and squinting as my eyes adjust to the dim light.

"In the back!" Coleson yells.

I walk to the back of the small two-bedroom bungalow and nod at another deputy who has been tasked with going through the kitchen. She wears gloves and moves a paper envelope to another stack of mail nearby. The worst part about some cases is when we have to sift through the mail or look through personal things to get a hint about whom the victim interacted with. You can tell a lot about someone by their mail. If they're in collections, they have money problems, and you can usually start pecking away at people they owe money to. Gambling debts are also an option there. Credit card statements, either paper or electronic, are also helpful, especially if the charges go to an awful lot of liquor stores or shadow escort services.

Basically, I'm here to snoop.

"Present," I say, an obnoxious lilt of sarcasm in my voice as I step into Portsmith's bedroom and greet Coleson.

Coleson doesn't find me amusing. "Get in here. I need to go interview a witness. I need you to take over."

"Has forensics already been through?" I ask, looking around at the mess in the room. I'll never understand how adult men don't clean up after themselves.

Coleson sniffs and snaps off his rubber gloves. "Yeah. Avery printed anything she could. The inches of dust around the joint easily showed where people touched, so that was helpful." I look around and see what he means. Dead bugs litter the windowsill, never wiped away after their demise. "Nothing out of place here. Avery says the place is just messy. No signs of struggle or kidnapping. She took some samples as a precaution and ran the light over everything, but she doesn't think anything happened here. No evidence of blood or body fluids not associated with the usual jerking off on the bed."

"You said you have a witness?"

Coleson pulls his phone from his pocket and taps on it. "Yeah. A woman named Angela. Didn't want to leave her last name. The news with Portsmith's picture is all over. This Angela says she saw someone matching that description outside of the drugstore on Fourth Street last week. Kind of loitering. She only remembers him because he was in the middle of the sidewalk annoying everyone. She said she saw a woman approach him."

"A woman?" I ask, freezing mid-glove up. I pause for another moment and then pull the rest of the glove on with a snap.

"Yeah. She couldn't remember which night it was because she works nearby and is always on that road. That's all she said in her message, so I'm going to go talk to her. See if she remembers anything else. I need you to look around here without fucking anything up."

One of these fucking days, this man will stop treating me like I'm a moron. Until then, I'll smile and act like it doesn't bother me. It only bothers me when we're on a scene and other people are around.

"Will do," I say with a fake smile.

"Great. I'll call in a bit and see if you found anything."

I give a mock salute and then subtly put up a middle finger when his back is to me. There are no mirrors in the room, or I wouldn't risk flipping him off, and the only other cop in the house is rifling through the kitchen. Great. I get the fun of the bedroom, which is literally where the magic happens in most of these cases. I have countless stories of sticky porn magazines, old porn DVDs from the nineties, and more than one used condom is usually found on site.

I get to work, shuffling through stacks of paper. After going through one stack, I head to the kitchen and chat with the other cop here to see if she's found any mail items. No such luck so far except for several lawn service flyers and a political mailer. So far, all we know about him is that he votes libertarian and doesn't mow his own lawn.

I search the bathroom, find the obligatory porn magazine under the sink, and I shake my head, thankful every day that Dwyer is adamant we search houses with gloves on, even if the crime didn't happen at that location. I find condoms in the medicine cabinet, but nothing is unusual about Jake Portsmith's hair or skin routine for a single male. There is only generic shampoo from Dollar General in the shower and some Irish Spring on a soap dish. Nothing here screams there's even a girlfriend around. Girlfriends or frequent female visitors would mean body wash, sponges, a second toothbrush, and more than two-in-one shampoo. This guy didn't have regular guests.

I leave the bathroom and am just about to take the gloves off and call it a day when I pass a small room that looks like a closet. Opening it, I find a washer, dryer, laundry sink with a container of stain stick on the ledge, and a large basket of what appears to be dirty clothes. Leaning forward, I quickly confirm they're dirty from the smell wafting from the hamper.

"Jodi? Did you check the laundry room yet?" I yell to the other deputy.

"Haven't got there yet, Kyle," she calls back. She moved from the kitchen to the living room a few minutes ago and mentioned she would go to the garage next.

"OK. I'll search here!"

I open the machines and notice the musty smell of wet clothes from the washer. This has been here since before the guy died. Nice to know I'm not the only one who forgets to switch clothes from time to time, but this seems excessive. They may have been here a week before he even died. Judging by how full the basket is, he was due a long laundry day.

I comb through the clean clothes in the dryer and empty his pockets. Nothing. Moving to the dirty basket, I go through and pull out his dirty underwear first, cringing as I set them all in a pile. It's better if I get them out first in case one touches my skin above my glove while I'm rifling through pockets. This isn't my first rodeo.

I look through pockets and pull out candy wrappers, a few coins that I set on top of the dryer, and a cigarette lighter. At the bottom of the basket, I find a pair of jeans that looks like a nicer pair, something a guy would wear out for a casual night on the town, and pull them out. I find nothing in the back pockets, and there are only mint wrappers in the first front pocket I check. In the second front pocket, I find an ATM receipt.

With a sigh, I unfold the ATM receipt. Fifty dollars taken out a Saturday night ten days ago. I eye the washer. These pants were at the very bottom of the hamper, so that means Jake didn't do laundry for that long. Gross.

I quickly eyeball the receipt again and am ready to put it with the coins when something catches my eye.

The ATM Portsmith used was the one in Peter's club. Huh. I didn't even know Peter had an ATM installed. He must have because the address is the same as the club. I even pull out my phone and check the address to be sure I'm not confusing it with another nearby business. Chills move up my spine, and I squint at the information at the top of the receipt like I'm trying to make it rearrange into different numbers or even another street name.

He was at the club a few days before a witness says she saw him walk away with a woman. Surely, it's a coincidence. Lots of men go to the club. Hell, I went to the club before I got to know Cheryl, even before Coleson told me to watch the club when shitholes were dying several months ago.

"Interesting," I mutter, drawing the words out, a smirk lining my face.

It's against everything I was taught in the academy, and also against every ethic a policeman has, but I shove the receipt into my own front pocket. No need to bring Coleson into this or direct him to my girlfriend, her coworkers, or her boss until I know exactly what the score is.

At the end of the day, it's just an ATM receipt.

CHAPTER 11

Kyle

I lean against the ATM machine in Peter's club and reject a call from Dwyer. He's probably wondering why my cruiser is parked at the club again. I don't have the heart to answer and tell him I'm inside this time. For one, I never told him or Coleson about the receipt. I don't need the whole force up in here yet again and watching the beautiful angel currently on the pole.

She's for my eyes only.

Well, my eyes and the other ten men in the room during the day shift. They sure aren't my fucking coworkers, though.

A crackle comes through my radio, and I silence it. I told dispatch I was taking lunch, but I really came in to snoop and verify there really is a fucking ATM here. I was surprised to see it in the corner off to the side of the bar. I'm also here to sniff out why Troy Acox's friend said the last time he saw Troy was at the damn club. It's too much of a coincidence that we have two dead men who were both at this club within three weeks of their deaths. Portsmith was here days before he died. It may just be a coincidence of dirtbags, but it's the only thing they have in common.

It doesn't hurt that I get to watch Cheryl dance.

I lean against the machine, sip the water I'm holding, and marvel at her as she dances to "Pink Pony Club" and does a perfect martini spin before climbing the pole so gracefully that I realize she probably has better upper body strength than half the county sheriff's office.

Better yet, she does most of it with her eyes closed like she truly loves her job. Maybe she likes some aspects of it. She loves to dance, but she hates the way men grunt at her. She told me that on our day trip to Chicago while we were hanging out by Lake Michigan. The only upside of the men at her job is the dollar bills they stuff into her outfit. She likes it because it feeds her boys, not her ego.

I wait until the song is over and Cheryl comes down from the stage to ask the men if they'd like a dance. My cock twitches at the thought of her dancing for me, but I can't deny that something visceral makes my stomach drop when I think of her dancing for another man. I think of her as my girl already, but I'm conflicted about her giving other men lap dances. One part of me is jealous. The other part is turned on that other men desire her.

She doesn't see me at first, and I slink panther-like out of the shadows into the middle of the room, my eyes watching her until she leaves a potential customer and takes a step toward another. She freezes mid-step when she sees me, and an awkward smile lines her face. She lurches a little like she wants to run to hug me, but she stops herself, her eyes darting left and right as if remembering we're in a strip club.

I close the gap and stop three feet from her, a respectable distance for any man in a strip club. The man sitting a few yards to my right visibly stiffens, and his hand tightens around his drink. It could be because Cheryl was on her way to talk to him but stopped to talk to me. It could be because I'm in uniform.

"Hi," she says.

"Hi, baby," I say in a soft voice, trying out the term of endearment. It feels natural, and she blushes like she's pleased.

We stare at each other for a moment, and I lick my lips when my eyes finally move away from her gaze and run the length of her. Her legs are bare so she can climb the pole. Only a black G-string with ties on each hip covers her below the waist. She wears a crop top with a strategically placed hole between her tits, and her hair is in a long ponytail. Red lipstick and dark eyeliner decorate her face, and her shoes put her at just under my height.

"I'd like a dance," I say before I can think of the conse-quences.

She tilts her head to the side. "A dance?"

"Yes, ma'am," I pull a wad of cash from my wallet and hold it in. She eyes it and sucks in her breath. "VIP room?"

What the fuck am I doing? I'm supposed to be sniffing around for proof something about this place is connected to Acox and Portsmith.

She doesn't answer, only nods and walks past me. She grabs my hand and pulls me toward the stairs to the special rooms where fuck all happens. I quietly follow her up the stairs, feeling the eyes of the other men watching us. They may wonder why a cop is paying a stripper for a lunch suck or fuck. If they're jealous I'm taking them away from the floor, they don't say anything. They'll get over it. Another dancer will be on the stage in a minute.

Cheryl leads me to an empty room with a couch, a small table with a drawer, and low neon lights. It reminds me of a dim college bar but with a place to fuck. Part of me wants to open the drawer to see what's in there, but I suspect condoms and lube. I remove my utility belt with the county-issued taser and service weapon and set it gently on the table.

She turns to face me and steps so close that her tits graze my stomach. I hold the cash up again. "I hope you know I just brought you up here to get you off the floor and talk to you. I'll give you this just to talk if you need to make up the lost wages. I won't treat you like a hooker. That's not my intention."

"I know. But I wasn't going to charge you for anything you *did* want, Kyle," she whispers, giving a subtle chin jerk to the couch. "*Is* there something you want?"

"I just want to talk without those men down there listening. I'm on my lunch hour and wanted to stop by and see you. I wouldn't be opposed to a lap dance. You know…if you have to conduct business to be in this room."

"Have a seat."

I sputter a laugh. "You're serious? You're going to dance for me? I was half joking. I don't want you to get in trouble if you're up here with your feet up."

"I wasn't joking," she says, a stern look lining her brow. She guides my hand holding the cash back to my pocket. "Your money is no good for it."

I take a couple steps back until my calves hit the couch, and I slink onto it, placing my arms on the back of the couch out of habit. I know the strip club no-touch rules during a dance.

Cheryl walks over to a place in the wall with a few knobs. I didn't notice it when I walked into the room, so it's well hidden if a police officer who is trained to be observant missed it. She fiddles with something and then walks back just as Madonna's old song, "Justify My Love," comes through a speaker.

My cock hardens immediately. We've kissed and held hands. I held her in my arms during selfies on Lake Michigan. I've seen her naked or her top pulled down when I was here at the club, but we haven't touched each other intimately yet. My heartbeat hums in my ears, almost drowning out the music. My blood quickens, and I yearn to wrap my arms around her as she starts moving to the music, her hair now down from her ponytail and skimming my chest as she bucks against me like she's riding me reverse cowgirl.

I sigh into her as she turns in my lap and gyrates, leaning back when she moves so that I can see the tops of her nipples if I look down her crop top as she arches away from me. She leans so far that she hooks one leg over my shoulder, grinds into my cock, and bows back so far that I almost reach out to catch her before she slides to the floor.

She doesn't slide, though. Her leg around my shoulders keeps her firmly against my embarrassingly hard cock. I admire her graceful movements that aren't clunky or stiff. She moves like water from one pose to the other, and when she purposefully unhooks her leg and slinks down to the floor, she moves cat-like into an all-fours move that puts her on her knees and makes my balls stiffen.

I grip the back of the couch and grit my teeth, mad with want and desire to touch her. I should say something charismatic and romantic. I should tell her how gorgeous she is on her knees. No, that's not right. I want this woman as a girlfriend. I should just stick with beautiful. Should I tell her she's athletic? Flexible?

"You're gorgeous on your knees in front of me," I whisper.

Fine. I went with pervert.

Her eyes darken with want, and I know I made the right choice. She wants me as much as I want her.

Her hands are at my thighs and rub from my knees up to my cock. She doesn't actually touch my dick, but she hits every inch around it, even forming her hands in a triangle around my cock as she massages me all the way back to my knees. When her hands slide back up, her fingers toy with the buckle on my pants.

I don't move. I only watch. When I don't stop her roaming fingers, she undoes my belt and then unbuttons my pants. The sound of my zipper coming down is deafening as the music merely becomes background noise. I hardly notice it since I'm so focused on everything she does.

She pulls my pants down enough to get to everything important, and I lift my ass a little to help her pull them to just above my knee. Kneeling as close to me as she can, her breath hits my legs and moves up until she pulls my cock out of my underwear and grips me at the base.

"What is it you really want right now, Kyle? Be honest."

"To not have my arms on the back of this couch so I can fist your hair while you suck my dick."

She smiles like the answer pleases her. "I give you permission to touch me, Kyle. Always. Only you like this."

That's all I need to hear. No other man to touch her in the VIP room. No other man to take her to dinner. No other man's dick in her mouth. I buck up a little and touch my cock to her closed lips. She giggles again and flicks her tongue out, teasing my head.

I force myself to sit still and not buck. She'll come to my dick when she's ready to suck it and not until. Thankfully, she opens her mouth and takes the first inch of me into her mouth, sucking lightly to start.

My eyes roll back in my head. I'm sure of it. I let out a sigh like I've been holding it for ten years. It hasn't been that long since I've been sucked off, but relief pulses through my body and down to my toes. I suddenly become aware of everything like he vibration of the music and her warm tongue sliding over my length. My lungs burn with the smell of her perfume, vanilla with a hint of cherries. Or is that lavender? Whatever it is, her sweet smell fills my nose. I take gulping inhales, run my hands through her hair, and hold it back from her face as I lightly pump into her mouth.

She bobs over me. Every time she moves down my shaft, every muscle in my torso and legs clenches. A moan escapes my lips. I roll my neck against the back of the couch, lost in the rapture of watching this woman bring me to full release.

"Just like that, baby," I say when she goes deep and speeds up. The combination is mind-numbing. I can't think. I can't feel anything but her mouth on my dick and her hair in my hands. "There."

She backs off to tease me and licks up and down, humming as she goes. When she goes back to doing what she was doing, I reward her by cupping her face and caressing her cheeks with my thumbs.

"I'm almost there already. You look so gorgeous with my cock in your mouth. Swallow me?"

Please swallow. Then again, I'd take a spit out just to see my cum dripping from her mouth. As it is, she's already drooling as she sucks. A line of spit dangles down to my balls. But every man knows the wetter and sloppier the blow job, the better it is. Cheryl must know men like women to drool and dribble all over their cock and balls, so she doesn't hide it.

I grip her hair harder and pump into her as I chase my orgasm. I want to watch her, but I squeeze my eyes shut as tremors take over my body. My balls tighten in release. A heavy load of hot cum fills her mouth, and she doesn't shrink or retreat from it. She takes every drop of me as I curse and mumble her name.

When I'm finished, she takes one long lick up my already-softening length and hums a little as she cleans me off. Swirling my cum in her mouth, she then quickly opens it to show me that my load rests on her tongue, waiting for me to approve it. I nod and watch as she swallows me with a loud gulp.

My cock twitches again. It was just satisfied, but the way she smiles up at me and worships my dick like it's a god makes it want another go. But a blow job is one thing. I won't fuck this woman for the first time in a gross strip club VIP room, no matter how much my cock protests.

I run a finger up her cheek and move back to her hair. Twirling a strand, I quickly cover my cock with one hand and watch as her face falls.

"Did I do something wrong?" she asks.

"No," I whisper in a husky voice. "I don't want our first time together to be in this room. If we were at my house, I'd already have you in my lap and riding my dick. I think what we have is special, and I want to keep it that way."

Something shifts in her eyes so that they light up for a moment and then dim the next. Does she really think she's not worthy of me because she's a stripper and I'm a cop? I adore her, and I want her to know I'm in this for the long haul, no matter her profession or if she's already a mother.

"But if you think I'm going to let you leave this room and go back downstairs to dance on that pole for other men without marking you as mine, you're insane." I move my finger back to her chin and tilt her head so she can't look away from me. "Take that little G-string off nice and slow for me and then come sit on my face."

I watch the words land, and they rattle around in her brain for a few seconds before she looks at the door and gets off her knees slowly. While she stands, I quickly buckle my pants into something that will force me to behave and not pull her back down to ride my dick when she's done coming on my tongue. I'll be tempted, so it's best to close up shop entirely.

She flicks her gaze to the door and then back to me, and we hold eye contact as I turn to the side and lie back on the nasty couch. I'll worry about germs or how many people have fucked on this couch later. All I care about right now is getting a taste of her and licking my way up and down her wet slit.

She takes my direction of *nice and slow* to heart as she runs her hands down her thighs and then slowly moves them up again until her fingers whisper at the tiny piece of fabric at her waist. She doesn't pull them down, but she unties one side and lets the fabric fall on its own. After she unties the second side, her panties flutter to the floor like they're nothing more than a feather. She lifts her top off next, and I lick my lips at the idea of her nipples in my mouth. Cheryl stands in front of me bare, watching me as I drink her in with my eyes. Looking for my approval, perhaps?

"Don't make me wait any longer to taste you," I whisper, crooking my finger and directing her to climb up my body.

She doesn't worry about my radio or my badge pinned to my uniform. She kneels over my waist and then knee walks up my body until that bare, glistening pussy is an inch from my mouth. When I look up, she's looking down at me, wonder in her eyes. Has no man ever done this for her?

Well, I'm here now.

"Stop hovering and sit the fuck on my mouth," I direct, reaching up to her tits and grazing my hands over them, cupping and gently squeezing. They're perfect for my hands. Filling.

She widens her legs like she's making sure she has enough room or I have room to breathe. I don't know. I'm only thankful the couch is wide enough for her to be comfortable.

Finally, she leans forward a bit, braces her hands on the couch arm, and drops her cunt onto my waiting mouth.

The earthy taste of her is comforting and titillating at the same time. I swipe my tongue from hole to clit, savoring the salt on my taste buds, and then swiping back to her pussy, swirling the tip in her warmth. I hum and hate that I won't fuck her here. My cock doesn't get the memo that we're behaving and is already fully hard again. I'll have to take care of that later.

Right now, I focus only on Cheryl and her pleasure. She whimpers when I suck on her clit. She groans when I flick my tongue over it. She positively melts, rocks, and cusses when I do both. I move between worshipping her clit and tongue fucking her pussy, but I mainly focus on the engorged nub that practically trembles against my tongue.

Lap. Lick. Suck. Suck. Tongue fuck. Lap. Lick. Suck.

She grips the arm of the couch harder and grinds over my mouth. She's relentless to the point that my entire face fucks her, my nose even grinding against her clit when my tongue is in her pussy. She wriggles into me, and I look up in rapture as I watch her tits sway.

Her thighs tighten around my ears. She straightens so she's not gripping the couch arms. Instead, she grips my hair and rides my face, calling my name over and over until even I'm almost tired of hearing it. She finally breaks apart, and my tongue is there, ready and waiting for the hot wet liquid that coats it. While I catch her wetness, she takes over rubbing her clit to completion.

When she's done, I help her slide over my clothing and extensive police accessories, and she flops forward onto my chest. I hold her there until my erection finally dies down enough to walk and until I know I can't get away with hiding from Dwyer much longer.

"I have to go," I whisper into her hair. "Dwyer said he didn't want to catch me in here."

"So don't let him catch you," she chuckles.

"That's what I always say," I say, smiling into the crown of her head.

"When do we go out again, Kyle?"

"Any time you want. My schedule is open for you, Cheryl."

"Even your lunch breaks?" she asks.

"Especially my lunch breaks."

CHAPTER 12

Cheryl

I don't have many great moments as a mother, but I'm a fucking hero today.

"Did you make this, Mom?" Jonah asks, cocking an eyebrow that looks so much like my own quizzical expressions that I almost startle because it's like looking into a mirror. He looks so much like Daniel that it's odd to see something of mine there. He stares down at the cake I made him, one for him and one for Jordan. I don't make them share birthday cakes.

"You told me what you wanted, and I couldn't find anyone who would decorate it," I say. "I bought a sheet cake, printed off pictures that I put on toothpicks around the edges, iced it, and did it myself. Is it OK?" My voice squeaks at the last word.

I worked through the night to make the cakes special. Both boys read manga, and there are some characters they enjoy. They wanted cakes with those characters on them, but every bakery in town looked at me like I had three heads or sounded very confused over the phone when I tried to describe what the boys wanted. I didn't want to disappoint them when I feel like I fuck up constantly, so I spent the evening gluing pictures onto toothpicks. That went about how I expected, and I cussed more than a sailor, but it got done.

I slice a piece for Jonah, slice a piece of Jordan's cake for him, and slide both pieces onto their respective plates before waving the knife at Lenore. "Chocolate or cherry chip? You have your choice."

"I'm a cherry chip girl and haven't had it in years," she says, smiling enough to show the gap between her front teeth. "Bring me some of that, honey."

I set the slice down in front of her and watch as she helps herself to my ancient coffee pot. You need something to cut through the sweetness of cherry chip cake, but the overwhelming sugar doesn't stop me from slicing my own piece.

I'm lifting the fork to my mouth when a knock at the door startles me. I jolt so much that the bite of cake plops to my plate, and icing splatters a little on my shirt. I immediately round the table and take the few steps to the door, my head cocked to the side. "Who could that be?" I mumble.

Both boys and Lenore dig into their desserts while I walk to the door, fling it open, and find a wet Kyle Mitchell standing at my door with two gift bags.

"Holy shit, Kyle, you're soaking!" I wave him inside, and he shakes the rain off his police jacket. "But you're just in time for cake." I eye the bags in his hands, one royal blue, the other gray. "Did I tell you it was the boys' birthday?"

He smiles at me and then nods hello to Lenore and the boys, who are all watching him with wide eyes like they've never seen a man show up in the living room like this. Granted, we don't get many visitors, but they still look like Jesus just came back, not like their mother's boyfriend stopped by.

Boyfriend? *Is* he my boyfriend?

"You mentioned it when we went to Chicago," Kyle says.

"You remembered that?"

"I remember everything you tell me, Cheryl. When it comes to you, I don't need to put it in my calendar. It was obviously a special day for you, and I won't intrude, but I wanted to bring something."

This is bad. This is a hazard of dating a police officer. If he remembers everything I tell him, he'll eventually catch me in a lie. I'm not all that great at remembering what I tell people. If I fuck up even little details like time, dates, or places, will he think I'm up to something?

Why the fuck am I dating a cop again?

Oh, I remember. It may have something to do with the fact that he let me sit on his fucking face after I blew him. That's never happened in that VIP room for me. Men take me up there, get theirs, and then leave me there.

But fuck...that mouth and the things it can do. My legs clench together at the mere thought of it, and I look at his lips before I can help myself.

If the boys were frozen to their seats before, the excitement of more presents is too much. They launch from their chairs at the same time and immediately grab at the bags.

"What is it?" Jordan asks, already pulling the tissue paper from the bag.

"Whoa," Jonah says as he turns the game cartridge over in his hand to check the back. He was quicker to pull the present out of the bag. "Thanks!"

I stare open-mouthed as the boys excitedly read the back of their games and then switch to show what the other got.

"Is that the right type of game for the console they have at Lenore's?" Kyle asks. "I can exchange them. I'm not all that up on video games that aren't *Call of Duty*."

"Looks like it," Lenore answers before I can.

"I'll take Lenore's word for it," I say. "I don't know the first thing about video games. Do you want some cake?"

"I never turn down cake. What kind?"

"You have your choice between chocolate or cherry chip."

"I'll go with chocolate," he says, already walking to the table and pulling Jordan's chair out. My son's cake was mostly eaten, but he's now too busy fawning over his new game. I doubt he'll be back.

I quickly cut a piece of chocolate with shaky hands. I can feel Lenore's smile on me even with my back to her. She approves of Kyle, and I know she approves of me having someone. Kyle didn't have to stop by today to celebrate the birthday of kids that aren't his, but he did anyway. He stopped by to show my sons he cared about them. He stopped by to show me he cared about *me*.

Nothing has ever made me want a man more. My entire body hums and not the way it did the other day at the club. This way is visceral. Feral.

I want to mark him as mine and only mine. I want my arms around him. My legs around him. I want him on top of me in bed, moving over me in a steady rhythm with his naked skin next to mine and his sweat dripping onto my tits and face. I want him to whisper into my ear, not only about what he wants to do with me physically, but I *need* to hear how much he cares for me.

For right now, it's enough he's showing me.

He sits in my crappy dining room chair I got at a garage sale and smiles as I place a piece of chocolate cake in front of him. He watches my every movement with hungry eyes. I know the look. It's the look I see at the club every single night. He's starving, and it's not for cake.

I move to the coffee pot as Lenore and Kyle converse about the rain, and I pour him a cup, desperate to please this man in any way I can. I set milk and my chipped sugar cup in front of him, but he ignores them, sipping his coffee black and asking Lenore about her garden out back he must have noticed from the road.

When the boys finally amble back into the room a half slice of chocolate cake later, Jordan goes to the fridge for a glass of milk, and Jonah flops into the seat next to Kyle.

"Do you like the game?" I ask, patting his leg.

Jonah nods. "Can we go over to Lenore's and use the console later?" he asks.

"Of course, honey," Lenore answers for me and gives me a sly wink. "As long as it's OK with your mama."

"I don't know, babe. You're over there a lot. I don't want you to intrude."

Lenore widens her eyes to what I'd call crazy eyes and subtly jerks her head toward Kyle. Kyle, for his part, innocently sips his coffee. "Nonsense, honey," Lenore says. "You know I love your boys. It's their birthday. They can come over." Her eyes widen to the size of dinner plates. I didn't think they could get any bigger. "All night if they want. I'll even feed them some frozen pizza."

Subtle.

Before I can answer her, Jonah immediately launches into questions about the game Kyle bought him, asking Kyle about certain characters who sound like foreign concepts to me. Kyle answers any questions he can't answer with, "I don't know, but let me look it up real fast." Kyle smiles and leans toward my son, showing Jonah that he has his full attention. Jordan, without a seat at the table now, walks to the spot between Jonah and Kyle, continuing the conversation, and I practically gasp when Jordan props his elbow on Kyle's shoulder like he's casually leaning against a wall.

Never, in the years I've had sporadic dates, have I ever seen my son touch a grown man. No handshakes. No shoulder pats.

Hell, I don't think I'd ever seen him do that to his father. Daniel never hugged the boys when he picked them up.

Dear God, are my boys starved for male attention from a father figure?

Kyle doesn't shake it off or even bat an eye. He includes Jordan in the conversation and even pulls out his phone and pulls up some of the characters they rattle off to him. For ten minutes they fall into easy conversation as Lenore and I trade glances over our own coffee mugs.

Eventually, the cake is licked clean from the plates, literally in the boys' cases, and the last of the coffee is finished. The boys pull Lenore out of her seat, and she gives a wave over her shoulder as she laughs her way out the door with the boys. They take the game cartridges, and I almost stop them with the thought they should take their toothbrushes, but that may be too obvious.

The door shuts behind them as they trot down the steps and across the lawn to Lenore's house. When I turn to face Kyle, he's already pulling on his still-damp jacket and patting his pockets to make sure he's got everything. But his eyes are dark with want, and I can't let him leave like that. I can't let him leave like that for my own filthy reasons.

"Stay," I whisper, peeling his coat down his arms. "Stay with me."

Chapter 13

Kyle

As soon as Lenore takes the boys to her house for the evening to play their new video games and her fingers have whispered my police jacket over my biceps, Cheryl is in my arms. She leans her head against my chest and snakes her arms around my waist. "Thanks for being so nice to my boys. Most guys aren't like that. I mean, I've never introduced them to someone, but I never found someone I felt like I *could* introduce to them. I hear horror stories from other women."

"I've always wondered why men do that. I mean, I get it that they think being a stepdad or something to another man's kids is an ego punch, but when you love a woman, you love all parts of her. They're part of you. I know you're a package deal, and we don't have to have this discussion again, OK?"

Shit. I said the L word. Will she pull away?

If anything, Cheryl practically swoons into me like she's relieved. She looks up at me with watery eyes and nods before standing on her tiptoes and kissing the very tip of my chin. I smirk and drop my head until I catch her lips with my own, tasting the cake she had earlier. I should have tried the cherry chip. The flavor suits her.

"Stay with me tonight, Kyle," she says as soon as our mouths part. "You never agreed to stay."

"The boys will be home later."

"They'll stay at Lenore's until late enough. Then, she'll use the key and let them in when it's time for bed. She does that when she knows I'm tired or when I work late but will be home soon." She pulls out her phone with the cracked screen to check the time, and I make a mental note to work on getting her a phone upgrade. "We have a couple hours at least. They have their new games."

"A couple hours?" I say, my hands already lifting the fabric at her lower back. "I could probably do it in five minutes. What are we going to do for a couple hours?"

She laughs, and my balls stiffen just from the sound of it. It's not her usual tinkling giggle or the laugh like I made a funny joke. My joke was bad, but maybe it's the idea of all the things we can do for fun over the next couple of hours. Touching. Exploring. Pushing our respective boundaries.

Her hands move to the hem of my shirt, and I raise my arms to help her pull it over my head. She holds onto it instead of tossing it onto the floor. Spinning and waving over her shoulder, she beckons me to follow her to the back of the house to a small bedroom behind the kitchen.

I look around Cheryl's room in the dim light with the eyes of an interested man. A woman's room gives away many things, and hers is no different. It's minimal, as I expected, with a full mattress on the floor that is also decorated as well as you can decorate a mattress on the floor. She has a small homemade headboard against the wall, and fluffy pillows are strewn around the bed and floor, giving the room the feel of an exotic harem bedroom. She's even painted the walls a robin egg blue to lighten it up. There's a small dresser in the corner and a tiny closet with a shoe rack hooked over the door. All in all, it's cozy.

She notices my interest in the open closet door and shuts it. "Sorry. I didn't know I'd have company."

"You live here, Cheryl. You're allowed to exist in your house."

"Sorry about not having a proper bed."

"It doesn't matter."

My heart skips a beat because I bet anything that the boys have better furniture in their room. She's that type of mom. Every kid should be so lucky to have a mom that does her best every day.

A set of blinds covers the double window, and she pulls the cord to shut them, leaving the room even dimmer now that the streetlight outside is no longer helping light the room. Only a plug-in nightlight next to me gives off a soft glow.

She sets my shirt neatly on her dresser next to a framed picture of her and the boys at a park and then crosses the room in two steps to place her warm hands on my naked stomach. My body shivers at just the touch, but it shivers even more as she squints against the darkness and presses her face closer to my chest. "What's this?" she asks, tracing her finger up a scar she can barely see next to the nightlight. "Childhood bike accident?"

I snort out a laugh. "No. Police work. Stuff happens."

She places a kiss on it, and I inhale, letting my shoulders relax and sink into her lips.

"What about this one?" she asks, moving down my stomach and noticing the circular pink scar near my belly button. The one there looks different than the rest because it's from using the old push-in cigarette lighter from my father's old Buick. I only did that once. The burn was a searing pain, not like the pleasant pain of a cut, and it simply wasn't as satisfying as slicing through my skin. There's something about knowing you can stop the wisp of the blade. Burning your own skin is trickier.

"Responded to an arson fire in Buffalo and got some sparks on my shirt button that got too hot."

She bends to place a kiss on it. I smile and run my fingers through her hair. "I have a scar a little lower if you think it needs attention."

She unbuckles my pants and looks up at me. "How did the one down there happen?"

"Knife."

That's not a lie. I just don't tell her it was my own knife.

"That's too bad. How'd I miss it the other day?"

My pants come undone, and she pushes them down until they loosely hang around my hips. I only need to wriggle and they'll fall to the floor, but I stay still. Gently gripping her hand, I bring it to the scar where my thigh meets my pelvis. My throbbing dick is a millimeter from her hand, and it's her turn to grin as she lightly runs the tip of her fingernail against it, toying with me.

"It's right here," I say, running her index finger across it.

I have a hundred other minuscule scars on my body, but there's no time to show her all my hiding places. I would have to show her the areas between my toes, behind my knees, and even in both armpits. Those are all some of my favorite places because they don't show evidence of my side hobby. In the case of my armpits, hair disguises the cutting.

She drops to her knees, a place I'm starting to love her being, and wraps her arms around my ass, gently kissing the scar I'm proud of the most as her cheek rubs against my cock. Then, she drops small kisses across the rest of my center until her mouth consumes me in one breath.

This time it's not hurried. I'm not watching the door and waiting for someone to use the room. I gather her hair in my fist and watch with hungry eyes as she takes me in and out of her mouth, slow at first and then speeding up before backing off again. I watch spit glisten on my dick in the dim light when she pulls back, and my balls throb at the visual show.

"You drive me insane when you do that," I whisper. "So damn good at it."

She opens her mouth and slides her warm tongue over the bottom of my cock before kissing the tip and smiling at me. "Good at sucking your dick or good at driving you crazy?"

"Both, but I didn't stay for head."

She bobs on my cock twice, and I hiss, pulling her hair a little in punishment that she's teasing me. She laughs in response, and the vibrations move from my dick to my balls. A small whine comes from my throat.

"I stayed to be inside of you. I stayed to see what you feel like under me."

"Feel like?" she whispers.

"What your breasts feel like against my chest as I fuck you close. What your legs feel like wrapped around me. What that tight little pussy feels like when I make you come."

She kisses her way up my stomach and chest until she's standing. My hand moves gently to her throat, and I hold her steady while I tilt her face to me enough to plant a long kiss on her lips that are plump from sucking me.

I pull her shirt off. Her bra follows. She helps me work her pants down. When we're both naked, I lift her, my hands palming her ass, and she wraps those legs around me the way I wanted until I lay her gently on the mattress. When I'm over her, I wipe a lock of hair from her face and then run my tongue from her neck to her ear, planting kisses on the way down her jawline. She wriggles under me, and I notch at her entrance, moaning when I feel how wet she is for me.

I slide inside her slowly, inch by inch until it's agonizing for me. I make her buck and pull my ass into her as she swivels her hips, urging me to thrust.

"So greedy tonight," I tease.

Using her legs, she grips my waist harder, and I can't stand it any longer. Her wet heat already has me trembling. Being wrapped up in her in so many ways is too much. I pump hard, and she whimpers with both pleasure and a little pain because I really went all the way. She grips my ass harder, though, so I push again, this time shallow.

Over and over, I push into her tight warmth, my head whirling. I squeeze my eyes closed and rock into her as pleasure moves to every inch of my body. It lingers in my abdomen, and I force myself to think of other things as I hold out for her. I want her to come first, and I want to do it like this instead of with my mouth so I can feel her orgasm creep into my balls and up my back.

"Do you have a vibrator, by chance?" I ask. Please, fuck, let her have one. I should have jerked off before I came over because I'm going to blow too fast if I can't get this amazing woman off in about two minutes.

She quietly nods, not at all put off by the question. "I've never done that before," she says, reaching toward the little table near the bed. "I've wanted to try it. I just never was with someone who...cared."

"I care," I say gruffly. I grab the purple vibe she pulls from the drawer. "You've got me so worked up, I need you to come, or you're going to tell all your friends I was a pump and dump."

She smiles and moves away from me. I almost object until I realize she's turning and getting on her hands and knees.

"Fuck, yes," I grunt, quickly nudging her legs apart and notching her from behind.

At the same time that I slide inside of her, I turn the vibe to the low setting and reach around, placing it at her clit. A guttural moan comes from her mouth, followed by a drawn-out cuss word.

"Yeah?" I taunt into her ear as I lean forward. "Tell me how good it feels to have that at your clit and my cock buried inside you."

She doesn't tell me. She just squeaks a little as I thrust and push her down on the bed with ever movement. She takes over holding the vibe, but she bites her pillow below me as I thrust hard, now knowing I can push her to the brink.

She squirms and moans under me as I take her. When she can prop herself up on one arm, her tits sway below us with my thrusts, and I long to grab them. Cup them. Hell, I really need to put it on my list to fuck them. But I busy myself with holding her hips, gripping until I'll probably leave marks. Her body bent before me is a glorious thing with her perfectly round ass and sculpted back. I watch her ass move with each thrust, and I bite my lip to hold off coming.

Finally and blessedly, her thighs stiffen under my fingers. She bites the pillow again and bucks back against me until she's fucking me more than I'm fucking her. "That's it, Cheryl. I feel that. I'm going to go with you."

My eyes shut, even though I try to hold them open to watch her. My body betrays me, and she gives one last moan before her body convulses in my hands. As soon as the first tremble causes her to clench around me, I'm already cussing and pushing into her faster and harder until my cock twitches inside of her with my release.

We collapse onto the mattress, and I quickly turn her to face me, switching the vibe off. I kiss her damp forehead and cheeks, and I set the vibrator on her pillow. Maybe we'll need it for round two, and I fully plan on having a round two that is harder and longer.

"Will you sleep with me tonight?" she asks in a whisper. I hear the tremble in her voice. She's worried I'll say no or will get up and leave her.

I wrap my arms tighter around her and pull her to my chest. I like the feel of her warm cheek against my side, and I like it even more when she trails a drowsy finger over one of my longest cutting scars. A surge of pride fills my chest that she's noticed it and noticed what I do to my body, even though I lied and told her the scars were from police work.

"I'll stay as long as you want me to stay," I say in a tone matching hers.

I kiss the top of her head for several long minutes, moving between it and her forehead, until her finger stops moving over my skin, falls still on my stomach, and slow, even breaths come from her chest.

"My girl," I say, giving her one last kiss on her forehead before closing my own eyes and drifting into sleep without nightmares for once.

Chapter 14

Cheryl

There are a few clients no stripper wants to fuck with, even if we cover our disdain with a smile and a lap dance. Bachelor parties suck and are a good way to go home sore after every single bro wants a dance. They're also loud and obnoxious, and you hope your bouncers are on point when they show up. Older men who visit the club alone are problematic because they're more likely to take a shine to a dancer that doesn't wear off after a dance. That's when you get your stalkers.

The other type of client to worry about is the average politician.

I've seen many clients like the man in front of me. They come in with a friend, usually a lobbyist or other political puppet master, and they throw money around, often demanding something we don't really do while blackmailing us they'll shut the club down if we don't do it. Peter, Lucy's cousin and the owner of the club, tells us not to do anything in the VIP rooms we don't want to do. Nice words, but not always realistic. There's been more than one girl who doesn't usually fuck clients caught riding them. Ironically, it's often a politician who ran on family values. A lot of the girls even call them "family value dicks."

I've seen the family value dick in front of me before, and chills move up my spine. I glance at the back of the room, but Rod is at the door, and he's the worst bouncer to deal with this kind of guy. Rod looks at his phone more than he watches the club. Charlie, the other bouncer working, must be on break because he's nowhere to be found.

From what I've heard, the county treasurer is a regular, but this is the first time his eyes have been on me. He wears a tailored brown suit, which seems an odd color choice if you're going to go through the trouble of commissioning a tailored suit, and his salt-and-pepper hair is slicked back like he's a thirties gangster. His eyes roam my body, not meeting my eyes. That's not surprising. To him, we aren't human. We're bang maids or warm mouths to enjoy while his wife waits at home.

"What do we have here?" the county treasurer coos, scooting forward in his seat. Next to him, a man in a red tie with pale eyes and pasty skin leers, his arms back on the top of the booth. Dollars litter the table in front of both men. I eye the cash and wonder how much of it is taxpayer money. "You up to show me a good time, sweetheart?"

My eyes move to the back of the club again. If ever there was a time for Peter to come out of the office and check things out, it's now.

"Sweetheart?" The county treasurer sticks a toothpick between his lips and chews, lifting his eyebrows in question. "I'd like a dance."

"I'm actually waiting for another client who wanted my time, but I'm sure another dancer would be happy to entertain you."

"I don't want another dancer. I think I like you. I'm Mark Ricord. Do you know who I am?"

Here we go with the old name recognition question, like I'm supposed to curtsy. I shake my head, playing dumb. I saw his name on the ballot during the last election, and I marked the other name.

"If you live around here, I'm your county treasurer. I make sure everyone, including you, pays their taxes."

"I'm not into politics." I avert my eyes, feigning looking for someone...anyone. "I've never heard of you."

He pulls a few large bills out of his jacket and sniffs the wad. "Too bad. I'm known as someone who gets exactly what I want. I want the VIP experience, and I can make your life easier if you make mine easy tonight." He jerks his stupid cleft chin toward the stairs. He's obviously been up there before and knows his way around the club.

I swallow, and my throat feels like glass. "I don't do that shit."

He scowls. "You'll do that shit for me. Like I said, I can make good things happen for you, but I can also make bad things happen."

I laugh. I can't help it. As soon as I sputter the giggle, he squints. His friend's eyes dart between me and the county treasurer, probably wondering if he should intervene. Perhaps he's thinking about the best way to do that. Ignore the situation like he's not seeing a common stripper turn down an elected official? Sit there and worry if it will mar the man's record before running for mayor or something else bigger than a simple county gig? Step in and bully me for the politician? Either way, the man looks around, probably making sure there are no witnesses. Once he's convinced we're not being watched, the man clears his throat and nods. Is that a silent signal that it's clear for Mark Ricord to do whatever he wants?

God, beta bitches make me sick with that shit. They're always covering for the biggest douche in the room. Even if they're not the perpetrators, there's the *not all men* shit they spew, all while turning a blind eye and coddling up whatever piece of shit they think is most important.

Anger burns its way up my spine, and the familiar urge to roll my neck is too much. I throw my head back and stare at the ceiling for a moment, closing my eyes and letting the music blaring through the speakers speak to me. My hair whispers down my back.

The man leans forward in his seat and smiles a maniacal grin. "Listen, sweetheart, you're going to go up those stairs with me, get on your knees, and suck my cock, or I'm going to find out exactly who you are, and you'll never dig yourself out of the tax audit." He glances at the two dollars another patron stuck in my G-string. "I bet you're not exactly on the up and up on those tips, are you?"

"Are you blackmailing me?" I ask in a bored voice. Murphy Beckett blackmailed me and even threatened the boys' lives. I've been tested by much scarier men than Mark Ricord.

His face remains neutral, bored even, but his hands are faster than I thought they'd be. His fingers pull at my hair so that I lurch forward until I'm flush with his body. My scalp stings form the sudden pain. Why do they always go for the hair?

"I told you what to do," he spits. "Now."

He spins my body and moves me ahead of him like we're simply walking up the stairs in a friendly manner. Would someone walking by think he's simply admiring my hair? I can practically feel his sleazy smile. His friend tags along behind us like a loyal dog as Mark Ricord pushes me up the stairs by my head.

No bouncers are nearby. The VIP rooms are checked when the staff feels like it, but my coworkers and I get away with a lot of illegal shit up here. It's possible Peter wouldn't find me for hours if the politician wants to get violent.

Once we're in the VIP room, he lets go of my hair and shoves me roughly to the ground. I stumble and catch myself, the rug burn from the cheap carpet already stinging my palms. At least I caught myself before I hit my knees. A stripper with rug burns on her knees raises eyebrows.

A leather dress shoe nudges my rib cage while I'm down. "Blow me, bitch, and dance a bit to make it pretty."

Ricord sits on the couch and undoes his dress pants before moving his tie to the side like he's about to enter a pie-eating contest. He places his arms on the back of the couch and jerks his chin at his friend who circles behind me. The man places his hand on the back of my neck. I can't go anywhere. The music is too loud on the stage. If I was going to scream for help, I should have done it while downstairs. I was simply too shocked.

The staffer pushes me along the floor so that I have to move unless I want to be dragged or get rug burns. I could handle one of the guys, even if it would be hard to clean up. But two? Vomit lodges in my throat, stopping just before it comes up. I gulp it down, and the hot wetness moves to my stomach. The staffer grabs my hands and forces them onto Mark Ricord's thighs. "Take his cock out, bitch," the man directs.

"Don't take his cock out," an unusually calm voice says from the door.

I know the voice well by now.

My body slouches a little in relief, even as hot shame makes me squeeze my eyes closed. The hands leave the back of my neck because another male has entered the chat. I send a little wish up to the universe that I heard the voice wrong. Maybe it's really Peter standing there. Maybe it's Kit, our bartender.

"Fuck off, Barney Fife," Ricord says. "Ruining a man's blow job can be bad for your career."

I open my eyes, mostly out of curiosity of how Kyle will handle being compared to the cop on *The Andy Griffith Show*, but I'm horrified when I find Kyle with a bored expression on his face and holding my usual favorite pink smoothie.

Odd. I never mentioned I liked those. It's my favorite one from Maud's, an out-of-the-way small business that specializes in smoothies and has the best mango I've ever tasted. Has he been watching me? Was he bringing me a smoothie in the middle of my shift?

"I don't think threatening my career is really the flex you want to go with here, sir," Kyle says in a soft voice like he's completely unbothered by any of this.

The staffer behind me sucks in his breath like his grade school friend who bullies everyone just got called out on the playground.

"Let's go downstairs and discuss this at the door," Kyle says, stepping out of the doorway and waving his hand toward the hall. "I'd hate to have to report this to my boss because you're harassing a woman at the club. That'll go over the police scanner, which is public, and the press may get involved. That would be a real shame."

I let out another breath. To hell with the press. Kyle's boss is Dwyer. He'd believe me. Lucy used to get into these situations. I know he'd believe me, even if Ricord has clout.

Ricord quickly stands, and I flinch, worried he'll hit or kick me, but I'm pulled to a standing position by the staffer, and my thighs are dusted by Ricord's puppet like he's showing Kyle I'm as good as new.

Ricord buttons his pants and straightens his tie. "I'm not leaving," he says. "This woman owes me something."

"Shit," the staffer hisses.

Kyle looks at me and back to Ricord. "Is that true, Bang?"

Thank fuck he remembered to use my stage name and didn't use my real one. I was nineteen when I picked that name, and it suddenly sounds so fucking stupid, but now is not the time to lament the dumb choices we make when we're young.

I shake my head and quickly scurry to Kyle. I don't touch him, even though I want to throw myself against his chest and cry or bury my forehead into his neck just so I can touch or smell something familiar. Instead, I stand behind him and shake. Shock maybe?

"He grabbed me by the hair," I explain, my voice shaking. "I told him I didn't want to come up here."

"Do you want to be up here with him now?"

"No," I mumble. I wrap my arms around myself, trying to stop my body from trembling. My legs shake like Jell-O, and I'm worried I'll fall. I gently lean against Kyle for balance.

Kyle sets the smoothie on a nearby table and waves his hand toward the door again. "I'll ask you one more time to leave."

Ricord's face reddens, and he crosses the floor in one second flat. His friend grabs at Ricord's belt, grappling against the fabric of the treasurer's pants in an effort to stop him, but Ricord is like an enraged bull with a red tablecloth in front of his face.

He gets nose-to-nose with Kyle and the men are so close that I wonder if they'll kiss. Why do men feel the need to get so close to one another when fighting? To touch each other while challenging dominance?

Kyle's hand presses against Mark's chest, but his face is oddly calm. Maybe it's from dealing with criminals as a police officer. I know Kyle's been in skirmishes and has taken down his share of runners, but Kyle doesn't blink an eye.

"Do you know who I am, son?" Ricord snarls through gritted teeth, gripping Kyle's wrist.

God, Kyle, just tase this mother fucker.

"I know who you are, Mr. Ricord. She said no. I'll escort you out, and that will be the end of it. No arrest. No press. Just walk out with me. We don't need a scene, and if you stay, you'll make a scene. She'll make a scene for you."

That's tempting.

Ricord looks around like he's finally realized he's in public and there are other people just downstairs who would see him escorted out by the police. His eyes flick to me and then back to Kyle before grabbing Kyle's hand and roughly swiping it away from his chest.

"You really want to tangle with me over a whore? I'll have your badge for this," Ricord whispers through gritted teeth.

Not really. I don't see Aaron reprimanding Kyle for defending me, especially when Aaron Dwyer can empathize with a stripper being picked on by a powerful man.

"Sir, I trust you'll do what you need to do, but I'm going to do what I need to do. This woman has asked you to leave."

"I'm asking you to leave, too," a voice says behind me.

I close my eyes and let out a long breath of relief. Peter doesn't come out of his office very often, but it's nice he has our backs when we don't want extra attention. I'll give him that. I wonder if he saw Kyle come up here with my smoothie and got nosy.

I turn to face Peter and smile at his sweatsuit and white tennis shoes. He looks like a middle-aged Florida man ready for a rousing game of bocce ball. But his jaw is set, and he nods at Kyle like he's silently pleading for him to get the elected official out on the street.

Kyle nods briskly and turns back to Ricord. "The owner has asked you to leave. Staying now would be a trespassing charge. I can take you in."

Ricord steps even closer to Kyle until their noses actually touch. I gasp, and Peter stiffens next to me, his hands clenched at his side. Mark's staffer friend grabs his boss's arm and tries to pull him back. "Sir?" the guy says. "We should leave. We don't need this kind of trouble."

If I'm nervous, Kyle looks positively unbothered. His face is a neutral expression of curiosity like he's curious what Ricord will actually do. Maybe Ricord knows there's nothing to be accomplished here. He would be trespassing and caught assaulting a stripper. Not exactly a good look for the next election.

Still, dick-slinging testosterone is a funny thing.

Ricord smirks and points at Kyle. "You're nothing." He points to me but doesn't look at me. He centers Kyle, somehow understanding that the young man with a badge is a bigger threat to him. "She's nothing. She's a whore. I'll find out who she is and make sure she's fined like a mother fucker if she's a day late with her taxes. And you're a toy cop who puts his big boy pants on every day to pretend he's the boss around here. You're not half the man Dwyer is."

"Absolutely true," Kyle says, deadpan. "But it's time to go."

"You'll never be anything bigger than a mall cop. She's a slutty piece of trash who's only good for a hot piece of flesh to catch my cum." He stares at Kyle's mouth since his eyes are level at it. Then, he points at Peter. "And this place is a shithole. I'll have all of you investigated for tax evasion, and I'll make sure the county looks at the books on this rundown rat's nest."

"Get this mother fucker out of my club now before I call Dwyer myself," Peter says, directing the comment to the staffer, who nods and pulls harder on Ricord's arm.

Ricord jerks his arm away but takes a step back, looking Kyle up and down like the man I'm starting to care about is nothing more than an insect. Maybe it's because Peter is here and upped the odds to two men on two men with an angry stripper thrown in, but sudden rage moves through me, right down to my toes, and I curl my hands into fists so hard that my trim nails dig into my palms. I feel the trickle of blood, but I don't notice any pain because my body is too busy shaking and trying not to lunge for Ricord's throat.

Insult me. Go ahead. I've been called everything in my career. Whore. Slut. Trash. Cum sock is a special favorite. But to insult Kyle? Fuck right off. This man does a lot for the community, and he's done a lot for me.

As much as I try to fight it, it's love. I realize that as I stand and watch Kyle stand his ground in this nasty VIP room. It's scary as fuck, but I'm falling in fucking love with Kyle and won't have him insulted, my boss threatened with tax consequences, and I won't be threatened.

I grit my teeth so hard they'd crack if I didn't take care of them. Peter must notice because an arm wraps around me. Handy if he wants to catch me if I go for Ricord's throat. Hell, maybe he's worried about Ricord's threat to have the state investigate this place from top to bottom. "Not worth it," he whispers next to me. "It'd come back on you. Let the police handle it."

Mark Ricord spins to leave and marches straight to the stairs, ignoring his friend who half runs after him on shorter legs. Kyle puts his hands on his hips and ambles after the pair, probably making sure they really leave, get to their car, and drive out of the parking lot.

As he passes, Kyle nods at me, probably giving me a quick goodbye, and I almost take his hand. I could ask him to stay. Ask him to come back and close the door, giving him something special for sticking up for me. Then again, he wouldn't take it this time. The urge to follow him is so great that I take a step after him, only for Peter to put his arm in front of my chest like my mother used to do when I was little and she'd brake hard in the car.

Peter's probably right. I should let Kyle do his job and make sure Mark leaves. Hopefully, the dickhead won't come back.

CHAPTER 15

One Week Later...

"Do you know what I find interesting?" I ask, touching the tip of the paring knife to Mark Ricord's chin right on his annoying little cleft.

He shakes his head, and a tear trickles down his left cheek. It's not like he can talk with duct tape over his mouth, though.

"I find it interesting that men like you think you're in charge or that you rule the world. In reality, the ice you skate on is thin, so precarious, that if we all stood up to people like you, every single one of your sandcastles would wash away. Only rich men like you and only men who are powerful deserve good things, right?"

Dickhead mumbles something under his duct tape, and his eye that's open and functional sheds another tear.

"You're just another little fucking pussy. A coward. I'm almost tempted to take that duct tape off and hear what you have to say."

More mumbling.

"Then again, I really don't care what you want to whine about before I gut you like a fucking fish." I back away and look him up and down, wondering where to start. Stomach? Throat? "Did you know what was going to happen today? Did you have it on your bingo card when you woke up this morning and put on your expensive little suit?"

I step closer, hearing the pebbles under my feet skitter. It's suddenly deafening in the forest with sounds I didn't notice when I pulled into the area. The cicadas are the constant white noise, while bullfrogs looking for mates punctuate the night every ten seconds. If I wasn't murdering an absolute piece of shit, I'd pull out a sleeping bag and stare at the stars until I nodded off to sleep.

When I'm an inch from his face, I push a lock of his hair off his forehead. The gesture is practically loving and the kind of thing a mother or father may do for a son. "But you don't care about anyone but yourself, do you? All that power you have over the county budget is the most important thing for you. I bet it's even more important than your kids, huh?"

I run my knife up his cheek and watch the blood ooze from the line. Panicked, Ricord shakes his head and yells as loud as he can around the tape. Well, his own sock is in there, too. I put it in before I taped his lips shut. He breathes heavily through his nose, catching his breath as he thrashes against the rope he's bound with.

"Did you really think I'd stop with you and wouldn't harm your family for the havoc you've brought to this county and state? Hell, this world?"

I really won't hurt his family. They're innocent, but dickhead here doesn't need to know that. I want his last thoughts to be worry, anxiety, and fear just like the women I now know he's assaulted and paid off, one even being a seventeen-year-old girl.

After the incident at the club, I looked into Mark Ricord's business dealings by asking around, and I don't mean the things going on with lobbyists and constituents. This man has fed more hookers in the Chicago area and surrounding counties than half the mafia. He's also paid off some women and has some pretty obvious non-disclosure agreements on the books.

I'm pulled out of my thoughts about his hookers and the odd foray into drug running by more muffled screaming. I laugh. "Who do you think you're screaming to?" I taunt. I hold my hands out and spin in a circle. "Nobody comes up here. Even if someone wanted to, the construction at the service road reroutes people. Nobody lives up here, and it's not hunting season. Who exactly are you yelling at? Me?" I point to my chest. "Do you think, after all the women you've bullied into fucking you or sucking your dick, I'm going to have an ounce of empathy for you and just let you go?"

Ricord takes a deep breath through his nose and nods.

"Why do you think I'd have empathy for you?"

He blinks away another tear and grunts something that sounds like, "Please."

"No, thank you," I say with a wide grin.

I drop the paring knife to the grass, and he watches it fall, his shoulders sagging with relief as it hits the ground until his eyes widen again when I sling my backpack off my shoulders. Squatting, I rifle through the bag in front of us and let him watch me get what I need. With each item retrieved from the bag, he screams into the sock and tape until the veins in his neck bulge and his face is bright red. He kicks at his ropes and even tries inching away like a worm that's been cut in half while I quickly walk to the car and retrieve the deer cleaning rack I found in my neighbor's shed.

"I borrowed this from a friend," I say, dragging the stand over to where Ricord sits. "Well, not really a friend. My neighbor had a stroke about six months ago. The family is trying to get rid of everything while the man is still in a nursing facility. They said I could have anything in the shed I need. You know, tools... A deer stand for gutting a local dickhead that likes to force young women into anal while his wife is at home with a newborn. I guess you didn't think I'd dig around and find out about Melanie Carpwright, huh? Well, the neighbors didn't say I could use the stand for that exact use, but that's what I took from the conversation. Funny how the universe sends you the things you need in life just when they'll be the most helpful."

I smile and brush dirt off my thighs as I drop the cleaning stand next to Mark, and I lean down to put the pins into place and secure the bottom so it won't fall over. Thankfully, I practiced at home and can get it put up in a matter of one or two minutes, even though I've never hunted a day in my life.

Never hunted animals anyway. People like Mark Ricord are a different type of hunting.

After it's set up, I reach for him, and he fights as well as he can with his legs tied and his hands secured behind his back. I'm impressed. The man outweighs me, but I still manage to get him upright after a weak headbutt from him. I laugh. The headbutt won't leave any marks because I was expecting it. It's what I'd do and have done in a close fight in the past.

I laugh in his face. "What are you going to do? Hop two miles back to the frontage road and hope you can wave down someone passing by at three in the morning? You're a dumb fuck."

He falls over and attempts kicking with both feet together. It's not hard to avoid the blows since his feet are tied. I get him upright again, this time closer to the cleaning stand, only to have him topple over a second time. Apparently, he's figured out that I can't get him on the stand if he's on the ground.

Pulling the hanger on the cleaning stand, I drag him kicking and screaming as far as I can. "Fine, we'll do this the hard way, Mr. Ricord." I hook the hanger behind his back, and the hook attaches to the ropes at his wrist. Ricord's eyes widen with fear as I quickly reel in the hanger line. When the pully stops because his arms can't go any further, I force it, turning the reel until I hear a sickening crack from Ricord's arms as they both break from the pressure. Muffled screaming fills the night. Even the frogs go quiet.

"Huh. I didn't think that would happen. Then again, the sticker on the stand says it can hold five hundred pounds. This must be for bucks or something. Maybe you shouldn't have fought so hard and this would be a lot easier for all of us. I could have just put your hands above your head the usual way, but no, we just had to do it backward."

I turn the reel, which is now cranking easier as the hangers move unobstructed. Soon, Ricord hangs from the deer stand, his arms completely bent into an unnatural position as his shoulders are dislocated. His feet dangle off the ground by only a couple inches, and urine soaks the front of his pants. Drops run out of his pant leg.

"Have you ever been hunting, Mr. Ricord?" I ask, securing the reel and then coming to face him. I inspect his tear-stained face, and his eyes are shut, probably ready to pass out from the arm pain. I slap his face. Hard. His head jerks to the side, and he whimpers. "I asked you a question. No passing out on me. You're going to be awake for all of this."

He nods.

"Hunting animals, I mean. I know you hunt women and like hurting them." I walk back to where I left my backpack items on the ground and pick up a notebook. "Lilian Chase," I say, looking Mr. Ricord in the eye as I pick up a bigger knife. Practically a machete. "You went to Northern Illinois, didn't you?"

He hums something I take as an affirmative answer.

"You and your fraternity brothers passed her around one night when she was drunk. Your buddies held her down. She was a virgin. You went first and then laughed that she bled. Told her she was a whore now and there wasn't anything she could do about it."

Ricord squeezes his eyes shut, and I walk to him, slapping him again to make him open his eyes. I then pinch his cheeks together until he winces, his mouth a grotesque O. "Look at me, you sick fuck!"

He opens his eyes. This time, I find what I want. Fear. He's scared. More urine seeps down his pants, and it combines with the smell of fresh shit. The smell of it is suddenly cloying.

"This is for Lilian," I say in a calm voice.

The knife moves so fast that I hear it cut through the air with a whistle. Ricord's ear falls to the ground with a squelching sound, and I step back to admire my handiwork and the knife's effectiveness, tilting my head while I marvel. It was a clean cut. Props to my new knife.

"Don't worry, I won't cut the other one off." I wave at my own ear. "I need you to hear me a bit longer. Now, you may be asking why I took your ear, Mr. Ricord."

He stares at me with wide eyes. The screaming has finally stopped. Maybe he thinks he'll get out of this by simply listening and hoping I get bored when I've gotten something off my chest.

Fat chance of that. Rage and revenge are my best friends.

"She screamed. Her deposition, which was pushed under the rug by the Greek council and campus police all those years ago, says she screamed and screamed for you all to stop. It fell on deaf ears." I look down at the ear and the blood now staining the grass and chuckle. "Now *your* deaf ear has fallen. Get it?"

He blinks a set of tears, one from each eye. Apparently, he doesn't like my joke. I think I'm hilarious, though, and I chuckle for a good ten seconds. The eye that's bruised and almost closed looks like it's weeping with infection instead of regular tears.

I collect myself and reach for him, unbuttoning his shirt and pushing it aside as he whines. Once his skin is visible, I go back to the notebook. "Claire Hennestath. Fellow intern at the accounting firm in Indianapolis where you worked the summer after your first year of college. Remember her?"

Ricord looks down, sobbing.

"I had to really dig for this one. Word on the street is that you paid her off after violating her one night. I found the payoff proof, and a copy of a signed affidavit saying it was consensual that you handed to the firm to cover your ass." I lean close to his face and stare at his mouth. "Why would you pay her off for sex and make her sign something stating it was consensual? I don't know of anyone who pays unless it's a hooker. Was she a hooker?"

He shakes his head and sobs.

"So you paid off a woman out of fear. That sounds like you did something a bit naughty, Mr. Ricord."

He whines against the tape and tries to roll his shoulders. Another crack sounds when he moves them, and I shrug as the cleaning stand rattles but holds. It's meant to hold an animal over twice his weight, but the animal is dead by the time it gets here. I'm not sure what all this wiggling will do. I need to hurry this along.

"Here's what I think happened." I raise my finger like I'm giving a lecture. "You raped her. She was an intern, and you got scared the next day. Scared she was going to report it. So you had Daddy and some lawyers make a deal with her, knowing full well that if she reported a rape, she'd be judged just as harshly in our society."

I take a deep breath and try to stop my own tears. Rape and the fact that most victims don't report it hits home. Most people will never know the shame.

"You made it sound like she could ride off into the sunset with some money and a smile because so many women don't report rape or are scared to report it. Is that right? She was probably scared of never landing a job in accounting again, so she reluctantly signed it, tried to disappear, and put it behind her. At least that money was some justice and solace for her."

Sobbing? Talking? I'm not really sure how to describe the sounds coming from Mark Ricord's mouth as he tries to rationalize a workplace assault from twenty years ago around a sock and duct tape.

I palm the knife and notice the weight of it in my hand. It's got the heft of a dumbbell. I grip the hilt tight and turn it so the tip rests at Mark's sternum. "This is for every rape victim who's been paid off by a rich little shit because he knows they don't want to go to the police and be revictimized." I move the knife down his sternum until I reach his waistband. I barely whisper the knife down his body, but blood drips from the line in torrents I wasn't expecting. "This is for every woman who just wants it to go away. To move past it and maybe make you hurt financially in the process because that's the only thing they *can* do."

I unbuckle his belt, and his eyes widen in panic again. I unbutton. I unzip and strip his pants off until they bunch at his ankles. Then, I pull his boxers down and don't comment on what is in them. Thankfully, I have gloves on, and I hope he is ashamed of what a coward he is.

I glance down at his dick and purse my lips together. "Well, that explains a lot."

He sobs like a baby now. His chest heaves with his cries. Blood from his sternum runs down his legs and over his tiny cock.

I flip a page in the notebook. "Let's talk about Jill McMasterson now, shall we?" I hold up the knife. "I'll just warn you, this one is a doozy, and it may get messy." I look down at the page and raise an eyebrow. "More body parts may come off with this one. It's the least I can do for Jill." I lift his cock with the back of the knife blade and chuckle at it. "This is going to be the first to go, and you're going to watch it drop right off your pathetic little body. But then again, you know this Jill McMasterson business is messy, Mr. Ricord."

His face reddens as he yells as loud as he can into the deserted forest where he'll die tonight. Not one of the deer, bullfrogs, raccoons, or coyotes will come to his defense.

"Don't worry," I say with a grin. "It'll only hurt for a second. After all, there's not really much to come off."

Chapter 16

Cheryl

I glance at my reflection in the rearview mirror and pull at the bags under my eyes. "So much for good sleep," I mumble.

Rifling through my makeup bag, I quickly dollop some undereye concealer on the dark circles and then blend the color with a makeup sponge. Maybe it won't be that noticeable. When I'm dancing, the lights are low except for some neon, but it's enough for the clientele to see the important bits.

If Kyle Mitchell could keep his hands to himself, I may get more sleep. Sure, there's been an unspoken agreement to only spend a couple of nights a week in my bed together, but those nights are not exactly great sleep nights. Any mother can tell you that losing two nights of sleep a week doesn't equal great skin. It doesn't help that I've been tossing and turning from thinking about my new hobby. When I'm not sleeping, I'm up researching dirtbags that roll through the club and finding out their other indiscretions from public case files.

I toss the makeup bag back into my purse and grab my belongings as I get out of the car, careful when closing the door with my foot because my hands are full. I paste a smile on my face that is part real, part fake. It's real because life is good now that Kyle and I are becoming more official. We haven't really talked it out, but I don't think he's seeing anyone else. Part of my smile is fake because I'd rather be with Kyle than work today. Dancing for other men isn't my idea of fun, and I only continue to do it because my boys like things like shoes and food.

Coral's eyes are on her phone when I saunter into the club. I hold out a cup of coffee in a takeaway tray from the little local drive-up place we both like. I've known her for a couple years. Even if we're not best friends, we've been through a lot. She takes the cup, her eyes still glued to a news channel. A reporter says something I can't hear, and there's a red scroll on the bottom of the screen.

"What's up?" I ask, taking off my sweater and hanging it up on the rack near the door before walking to my assigned vanity area and pulling my makeup bag out of my backpack.

"Something bad," she says.

"Nuclear war?" I ask. "That asteroid that's got a small chance of hitting us in 2032 upped to total annihilation? At this point, we may want to consider it as a viable alternative to our timeline."

She turns to me and blinks. Why does her skin look gray?

Fear.

Coral and I were once forced to run drugs for Murphy Beckett. The pale color of her skin reminds me of how she looked when he threatened her. Sweat pools in my armpits, and my heart pounds.

"Seriously, what is it?" I ask.

"I think this is bad for the club."

"What the fuck are you talking about?"

"He came into the club a lot. I know him, Cheryl."

"Who?" I ask. "Who are we talking about?"

Oh, God. Coral somehow knows about Troy Acox. Wait. Jake Portsmith? The news reported it when both were found. Did they find a print? Maybe they found my hair and matched it to some DNA from my shoplifting arrest that I didn't know they collected. Did my coworkers remember who I've interacted with? Fuck, I need to stop picking off guys from the club now. I need another way to find dirtbags.

Coral flips her phone to show me what she's watching. It isn't the local news. Fuck, that's CNN. A picture of Mark Ricord is in the upper right corner, and the red scroll at the bottom explains he was found dead in a rural area about three miles away from my house.

"A county official is dead," Coral says. "I saw him push you upstairs last week. I also saw the police officer you like walk him out. Did he threaten you or Peter? If he threatened Peter, do you think the police will start sniffing around here?"

Jesus Christ, I hope not. Putting my own trouble aside, I squint at Coral, wondering exactly what the fuck she's so worried about with the police sniffing around the club. Is she still running drugs or fucking for money?

What the hell is going on around here?

My vision tunnels, and I grip the edge of the vanity so hard my knuckles go white. I quickly gaze at the phone, and Coral turns up the volume. She holds the phone up to her ear to hear better, but I'm going to be sick.

CNN. This is a national headline. Will this stay local for a local detective or even Aaron Dwyer to sift through, or will feds get involved? At the very least, the police are about to come sniffing through the club. Peter will have to tell him that Ricord caused a scene. Kyle will tell them about Ricord being escorted out. His staffer will give a statement about how Ricord threatened me. They'll know I was the cause of the scene. Will they find something that connects me to Troy Acox and Jake Portsmith?

Either way, this is getting too dangerous. I need to stop.

My stomach sinks, and tears prick my eyes. Fuck, it's cleansing to remove these dirtbags from the world. It's better than any therapy could ever be. I feel free, focused even, for the first time in my life. I'm a better mom because bad people who hurt women and kids are getting their karma. It's hard enough to be a mother and let your heart walk around outside your body, constantly worrying something will happen to them or they'll run into someone like Troy Acox, Portsmith, or even Daniel.

But I can't get caught. I'm dangerously close, especially if the police are going to look closer at the club.

What would Kyle think of me if I'm a suspect? I'd never hear from him again. Why did I introduce him to the boys? They love him. Now he'll leave, and I'll have to answer hard questions. Jesus, who will take care of the boys if I go to jail? I don't want him brought up by Daniel's parents. Lord knows they didn't exactly do a bang-up job with him.

I take a deep breath and focus on Coral's phone. Whatever questions she just asked me leave her mind as she focuses on the reporter's details.

I cock my ear and listen along with her. "The county treasurer was found dead two days ago," the anchor reports, her face grim but otherwise without emotion. "Forensic investigators say he'd been dead for days after he was reported missing by his wife. A volunteer search party found him in a field three miles from anywhere and hanging from what authorities are saying was a deer cleaning stand. Police have no suspects but do not think the general public should be concerned. All possibilities are being looked into, including the possibility it was politically motivated or something involving the tax code." The reporter drops her voice. "We'll have more information at the ten o'clock hour."

Chapter 17

Kyle

The sound of my phone vibrating on my nightstand pulls me out of a dream involving Cheryl in one of my T-shirts riding my cock. I grimace at my erection and then at Coleson's number flashing on my screen. Whatever relief I need will have to wait.

"Yeah?" I ask, my voice still full of sleep. Gravelly. I run a hand over my stubble. "What?"

"Mitchell, I need you to stop being lazy and get in here. We have some CCTV footage you need to review for Portsmith. We found a bodega with security cameras near where our witness last saw him, and we want to match them with traffic cameras between the crime scene and the bodega. I need you in here and reviewing these."

More video footage. If you'd told me when I was young that I'd have a job that would be fifty percent watching people buy gas station food, I'd have called you a liar.

"On my way," I mumble before disconnecting the call.

I run through the shower, quickly handling the erection thing as best I can with my mind on the fact that I need to be at work as soon as possible. I brush my teeth, slip into my deputy uniform, and grab my electric razor to use in the car on the way to the station. I don't bother with the sirens and lights, but I don't get caught in traffic like I'm sometimes prone to when people slow down at the sight of the cop car. It's one of the more annoying aspects of the job. Nobody drives with the flow of traffic with police around. It makes us late, too.

I walk into the bullpen and am immediately met by Avery. "You reviewing tapes?" she asks, jerking her chin in the direction of one of the evidence rooms.

"Has Coleson been barking for me?"

"Yep. He's horny to find something on them."

"How come you're not doing it?" I ask as she falls into step with me as I pass desks and even bypass the donut box. Avery picks up one with pink icing and sprinkles. I noticed someone, probably Coleson, started buying them for her. They were never in the snack lineup before. "I figure you'd want to catch this guy."

"Person," she corrects around a mouth full of donut. "Remember Troy Acox needed a bit more power with that chicken wire around his neck. I think it's a woman. Although, she must be strong and work out or something to get Mark Ricord into that deer cleaning hoist."

I stop and face her. "Do you think a woman got him in there?"

"Don't look so damn shocked or sound so damn sexist. A woman could get him in there. I'm little, and I think I could do it if I could get him hooked. The reel did the lifting. Rope marks on his wrists and ankles show me he was tied up when he was hoisted onto it. The killer probably hooked him onto the rope and only untied those after he was dead to display the mess they made of his organs. Whoever did this wanted to show off and shock us. She also had to untie him to skin him the way she did."

I frown and stare at the donut as she brings it to her mouth for another bite, not caring that she's eating and casually talking about a man being gutted and skinned. She may as well be talking about the Cubs game last night. I guess she has a strong stomach.

"You think these are related?" I ask.

She shrugs. "No idea. To answer your question, I only do the science report. Someone else does the finding out. You're on your own watching the Portsmith videos. That falls under detective work." She waves her hands in a shooing motion. "You go watch your videos while jerking off, and I'll go handle the science."

"You're mean as a damn snake," I say with a chuckle.

"Yeah, but you're creepy as fuck, and everyone says so."

I pause and lift an eyebrow. "Who exactly says that?" I ask.

This is all news to me. I thought I had a pretty good reputation here. If anything, people are overly nice, like they think I'm not very bright, which is kind of what I was going for.

She gives a half-hearted shrug and cracks the gum in her mouth. "People. Some of the veterans. New people like you OK, but some of the older people think there's something off about you. Don't kill the messenger."

"Of course not," I say with a smile, doing my darndest to not let it be a creepy smile. I want to be her friend. "Do *you* think I'm creepy?"

"Hell, yes. But don't worry, Kyle. I find you creepy in a charming way." She smiles a dazzling grin before flipping me off.

I turn away from her without asking for more info on how she thinks all these cases are related or even why I'm creepy. Maybe I have some scars I wasn't aware I left visible. I just file it away for later. I'll sit down tonight and write out ways I can work on that. I was just trying to be quiet, not make anyone uncomfortable, but I should rethink it. Now that Avery mentioned it, I guess people often think the quiet people are up to something.

I'd usually sit on this until I had a chance to be alone and cut to feel better, but I don't have that luxury right now. I bite my lip in frustration, and I pat my front pocket where my knife is. I glance at the webbing between my thumb and index finger and wonder if I could get a quick cut in and just pass it off as a simple papercut. Maybe Coleson would even give me a Band-Aid and a kiss.

Coleson's waiting for me, and if Avery had something to report, she would have said it. It's interesting she thinks the county treasurer and the other murders are related, though. Investigators who have looked into the most successful serial killers know that the killer should never choose the same type of victim twice, never use the same method more than once, and never dump in the same place to avoid being labeled as serial. Even if the killer is following the rules of avoiding being caught or labeled as a serial killer, Avery knows something is off about all of this.

I open the door of one of our evidence rooms, the room where we keep our video surveillance equipment, and nod at another deputy as he walks out of the room carrying a fast food bag and an empty coffee cup. Coleson spins in his chair and squints. "Glad you showed up."

"Shut up. I'm in early. Don't act like I knew you'd have footage for me to review and didn't show up."

He raises an eyebrow. "What's gotten into you lately? You've been talking back. You don't usually do that."

"You don't like that I won't take your shit anymore?" I ask with a shit-eating grin. "I want pink iced donuts with sprinkles, too. Maybe if I tell you to stick shit up your ass, I'll also get them delivered to me every morning."

His face reddens, but he can't help but smile. "Shut your fucking mouth."

"You're too old for her. What are you? Sixty?" I jerk my chin at his salt-and-pepper hair.

"About eighteen years off, Einstein."

"That's a hard forty-two, man. You look exactly like my grandpa."

"Come over here and do your fucking job," he growls.

I walk over to the monitor and set my messenger bag down on the table. He points to the screen of one video he's watching.

"What am I looking for?" I ask.

He taps the screen. "This is the spot we're looking at. It's across the street and to the right from Dryden's bodega. Our witness said she saw Portsmith talking to a woman, but she couldn't remember which night the woman approached Jake. I've been watching Wednesday footage, but I need to get some sleep. I've been here eighteen hours. You need to review Thursday and Friday for me. Call me if you see anything."

"Do you have the picture of Portsmith? I don't know if I remember what he looks like." It also doesn't help that Portsmith's driver's license had him sporting blonde hair and being clean-shaven while he had a bit of stubble and a bald head when he died.

Coleson taps something on a tablet and sets it in front of me. "Here, use this. His social media. The latest we have."

I nod and slide into the chair as soon as he vacates. I press the button on the video replay system, ready to catch footage of a woman with a strong enough stomach to burn a man alive. It takes a lot to kill someone, in general, but burning has the added sensory fun of smell. It's not for the squeamish. Not wanting to watch in real-time, I set the replay to move almost double. That should speed things up.

I let out a long sigh after watching the first five minutes of literally nothing happening. After ten minutes, my eyes flutter, working to stay awake. I send another beat cop to get me coffee, ordering a double shot to try to stay alert. All I need is Dwyer to come in and find me asleep.

Thankfully, the caffeine works through the Thursday day-time video. By the time the system gets to Thursday evening, other cops filter in and out of the evidence room, and I have someone to talk to. Lance Bessin drops off evidence from a home burglary and spends five minutes flipping through his weekend Tinder options. Once we swipe right on a few, we spend another ten minutes rating the women into first choice, second choice, and so on. Yeah, it's sexist and disgusting, but it keeps me awake. My mind flits to Cheryl, and I take a break, worried I'll get half a chub and not be able to do anything about it if I don't get other social interaction.

I pause the footage and flit around the bullpen, sitting on desks and chatting with some of the newer patrol grunts until Dwyer enters the area in a grouchy mood. Only then do I head back to the video and hope I can stay awake another few hours until Coleson returns.

As soon as I'm back in the seat, I click play and watch the grainy footage until a car that looks like Portsmith's vehicle rolls to a stop on the screen right where Coleson's finger was this morning. I'll say one thing for our detective, he listens to witnesses when they describe something.

I watch as Portsmith gets out of his car, walks into a cookie place across the street, comes out with a white paper bag, and then stands on the sidewalk as he scrolls his phone. He stands out of the way of passing pedestrians for a few minutes but then walks into the middle of the sidewalk. It's a nice day and Portsmith doesn't seem in a hurry. Is he waiting for someone?

I scoot closer in my chair and watch each person passing by the victim. Most ignore him and circle him. One woman gives him a dirty look for blocking the sidewalk before walking into the cookie store. Angela, perhaps? That makes sense since I notice a CVS bag in her hand, and she mentioned she had been shopping at the drugstore when she saw him. Was she inside the cookie place when she saw the mystery woman approach him? A homeless man nods, asks him a question, and then moves on when Portsmith shakes his head.

Another car passes by the frame and turns down the alley at the stop sign. I can't see the license plate since it's just out of the frame, but I know the make and model. I hold my breath as the owner doesn't get out of the car, simply sits in the car like they're watching.

I lean forward and squint at the screen before slowing down the tape to regular speed now that Angela is in the cookie shop and our boy on the street is about to be approached. I know it. After about ten minutes, I'm just about to fast forward again, but the car door opens. I watch as Portsmith puts his phone back in his pants pocket and heads for his own vehicle like he's decided he doesn't want to stand in the middle of the sidewalk anymore. He stops as soon as he sees the driver of the car in the alley.

I'd stop for her, too. In fact, my entire life has stopped for her in the past few weeks. I was hoping I wouldn't see what I hypothesized when I found the ATM receipt in Portsmith's pants, but there it is in grainy bodega footage.

I pause the tape and don't blink. Letting out a sigh and crossing my arms over my chest, I lean back in my chair and wonder how I'm going to record over the file before Coleson sees it or how I can tamper with it to account for Portsmith being on tape and then suddenly disappearing.

CHAPTER 18

Cheryl

I knock twice on the door and listen as Kyle shuffles closer, flinging the door open with a wide smile and leaning against the doorframe with hooded eyes. "Did I wake you?" I ask, holding out a box of pastries I bought at the grocery store after I got the boys off to school.

He shakes his head and waves me inside. "I just woke up." He stretches. "I was thinking of staying in bed, but letting you in was a good enough reason for me to get up. Do you want coffee?"

He doesn't wait for my answer. I follow him into the kitchen, eyeing his naked shoulders the entire way. My fingers flex around the pastry box because I'm tempted to drop it and run my hands up his muscular back. My body warms because it knows what it feels like to have my legs wrapped around those shoulders. My eyes roam down to his sleep shorts and admire the tight fit around his perfect ass. This man never misses back workout day. When he reaches into the cabinet to grab a mug, I nearly drool.

"What brings you by?" Kyle asks. He looks over his shoulder and grins. "Not that I'm not happy to see you. I could get used to seeing you every morning."

A blush creeps up my face and settles in my cheeks.

I can't tell him that the news has me spooked and I need to see his face. How do you tell the man you're dating and actually see a future with that you're concerned the police will suspect you killed Mark Ricord after someone points a finger at the club? I knew I needed to hear his voice when I woke up today. I need his arms around me.

But how to ask that without bringing attention to myself?

"Did you see the news about Mark Ricord?" I ask.

Kyle freezes with his back to me as he loads a coffee pod into the machine, and his shoulders tense for a brief moment before they relax. If I had blinked, I would have missed it. But I saw. I tilt my head and bite my lip, worry eating its way through my stomach.

"Yeah, the department is all aflutter with it." He shrugs and turns the machine on before turning to face me and leaning against his granite counter. "Out of our hands, though. State police are all over it because of who it is, but they're losing interest. Feds sniffed around at first but are leaving it to the state. Dwyer says they can't find any political motivation, though, especially without any viable suspects. It'll ultimately be up to

Coleson to find something about it. Looks like it was random or someone had a specific beef with him. It looks personal to me."

The machine stops and Kyle hands me a mug, his fingers brushing mine as he passes it to me. He turns back around and loads his own pod into the machine before answering. I take a moment to look around his kitchen, noticing how much better it is than my rundown house. Stainless steel appliances shine, so it's obvious Kyle takes care of his house. Copper pots hang from an overhead rack, and I smile, thinking of Lucy because Copper was her stage name.

Lucy, who once murdered a man who threatened the girls at the club...

"Nothing is certain, of course," Kyle says, pulling me out of thoughts of Lucy being a murderer who murdered shitty men like Mark Ricord. "But if he acts like he did at the club the other night around other people, I'm sure someone out there wants to take a pop at him. Swell guy." Kyle's voice drips with sarcasm.

"Did he say anything to you when you walked him out?"

Kyle grabs his cup off the machine as soon as it shuts off. "Just a sweet conversation between gentlemen. I told him I'd wait until he was in his car. He then called me a cocksucker and a low-IQ pig a few times. Is that what you mean?"

I grip the mug tighter, mostly out of anger that anyone would talk to Kyle like that. I can safely say Mark Ricord got what he deserved. Karma's a bitch.

We sip our coffee in peace for several minutes before Kyle circles the island in the middle of the kitchen and snakes his arms around my waist. This is what I need. I need him with my face pressed against his warm chest. I need him with his strong arms around me. His biceps flex like they know I'm thinking of them. Never, in my entire life, have I felt safer than I do at this moment. Whatever happens, he'll protect me. I know that deep in my core.

Speaking of my core, my body wakes up and yawns like it's been asleep since the last time I was touching him. He pushes his hips against me as far as possible, and I don't even have to slide off the chair to wrap my legs around him.

Leaving our coffee, Kyle walks me to his bedroom. We don't need words. We don't need any other signal. Are we getting used to each other's body enough that we know the signs?

What I need right now is for Kyle to fill me. Is it crass? Yes. Is it a short-term fix because I'll just have to eventually leave the safety of his bedroom and face the real world? Yes.

I'm here now, though. My legs wrap around him tighter, and his erection pulses at my center. He presses forward twice, essentially humping me like a teen, and pleasure shoots up my spine.

This time, it's not frantic. He lifts my shirt over my head and places it neatly on the bed next to us. My bra follows, and he bends to place soft kisses on both nipples before kissing his way down my stomach. No biting. No nipping. No filthy words this time. The only sound is the sound of his wet lips meeting my skin all the way down my body until he pulls my sweats down. He kisses my leg all the way up until he runs his tongue up my slit like he's saying hello.

My fingers wind through his hair as he kisses up my stomach. "I'm glad you stopped by today," he says when he reaches my neck. "I miss you when you're not around. I don't want to see anyone else, Cheryl. I hope you know that. I don't want to do this with another woman. Just you."

There it is. What I've been waiting for.

I nod, unable to speak, but my body speaks for me as I push down his sleep shorts and grip his ass muscles.

Kyle's fingers run through my hair as he places soft kisses on my cheek, up to my ear, and then down to my neck. "Promise me something, Cheryl." He breathes heavily as he says the words.

"Anything."

"Be careful. If you ever get into a situation you don't think you can get out of, you ask for help. I'll help you. No matter what. Got it?"

My stomach flips as he nips my earlobe, and I can't tell if it's him nuzzling my ear and notching his cock at my entrance that has me on edge or if it's because there's something in his voice. A warning? A promise to keep me safe?

"Why do you want me to be careful?" I ask with a gasp, my mouth opening as he gently slides into me and swivels his hips.

Above me, he smiles before throwing his head back and letting his eyes close in pleasure. "Because I'm so fucking in love with you."

CHAPTER 19

Cheryl

Lucy flicks off the lights in the pole room and then leans the Swiffer mop against the wall. Her eyes are tired, but she still won't leave the club until every single drop of sweat is cleaned from the floor and the poles are shining and sterilized.

"Long day?" I ask her as I switch from my class heels to my sneakers.

Being attacked in the parking lot after class will always be in the back of my mind. I need to be able to run when I have to get away. Never again will I step out of a building I'm working in without changing out of the stripper heels, even for a break.

She looks at the door behind me as if distracted and walks to it, flipping the sign to closed. "You have no idea."

Something is going on with her. She's been weird for about a week now. We've never been super close friends, but we bonded over getting rid of Daniel's body. Still, she was talking more for the last few months since it happened. Laughing more. Then, about a week ago, she just stopped. Like something upset her. She's rattled and not talking about it.

I stare at her, looking for things I may not have noticed because I've been too busy thinking about Kyle non-stop. Bags I've never seen before have set up shop under her eyes. Her normally bright skin seems pale and even discolored around the mouth like she hasn't been using makeup, even though I watch her apply it at the desk.

I set both feet on the floor and put my heels on the bench beside me. "Want to talk about it?"

She shakes her head and gives a weak smile. "No big deal. Family stuff."

Her listless grin reminds me that her whole persona has been weak the last few days. Her voice hasn't been as loud as usual. She doesn't eat much, and she asked me to take her Monday morning class. Something is definitely up.

"Is it Aaron?" I arch an eyebrow and lean closer, dropping my voice. "Do I need to handle him?"

I meant it as a joke, but Lucy looks at me with a startled look like she's horrified at the mention of it. I hold up my hands. "Joking. I'm just worried."

She runs her hands through her hair. "It's not Aaron. He's great."

"The girls giving you a hard time?"

Lucy's stepdaughters are always sweet whenever she brings them to the pole gym while Aaron is working. They sit at the check-in desk, aren't allowed in the classroom, and will sit and read or color. I had a full conversation with Pearl about *Harriet the Spy* just last week, and the child was excited and well-behaved. I can't see them as ball busters, at least not until the teen hormonal rebellion explodes, but Aaron and Lucy have years for that.

She sits in her seat at the counter and clicks off the neon desk lamp, casting the room into dim light. Only the standing decorative lamp by the door is still lit. "What's going on with *you?*" she asks.

"Me?" I shrug. "Nothing!"

We stare at each other, knowing full well we're both hiding something. Lucy rolls her neck, and I mimic her without intending to do so.

"Stop," she says, deadpan. "Something is going on."

Where to start? I can't very well sit here and tell her that I'm killing shitbags who visit the club and who admit to behavior outside the law. I've been trying not to bring up Daniel. I know I could talk about it with her, but we've kind of taken the unspoken stance that if we don't talk about it, it'll go away. I want to tell her that I reached out to Daniel's parents in Minnesota and asked them if they'd heard anything from him because the boys are asking and I haven't received child support. I want to tell her that I think that will help throw them off the scent. I'm just not sure how to bring it up.

"I really don't know what you mean," I say, doing my best to paste an innocent expression on my face.

"What's going on with you and Kyle Mitchell?"

I let out a long sigh, and my shoulders relax. Boys. I can talk about boys. At least, I used to talk about boys with girlfriends in high school before my life went nuts. In a way, I've been wanting to gush about him to someone, anyone, but I don't have many friends except girls like Coral at the club, and Lucy's husband works with Kyle. I wasn't sure it would be welcome.

"It's good. We've been out a lot lately."

"Has he met the boys?"

"Yeah. It wasn't an intentional thing that I thought too hard about. They don't spend a lot of time together, so they're not bonded if we stop seeing each other," I explain. Moms are often shamed for introducing boyfriends too soon to their kids, but Lucy doesn't scowl or widen her eyes. She's not shocked he's met them. "They get along. Kyle wants one child of his own."

That was a fun conversation the other night over a romantic dinner. I've been unsure about his interest in me, but when the guy you're dating asks if you'd be willing to have one more, you know you're on the right track. It's quick, but I *really* like him. Kyle is also at the age when he won't waste his time with a relationship if our goals don't align. It doesn't mean he'll breed me next week. He was simply asking if we want the same things. I took it as a good sign.

Lucy leans forward. "Do *you* want another child?"

"With someone like him? Hell, yes!" I say. "It's always been in the back of my mind to have another one if I meet someone I love. I just never thought it would happen because of what I do for work, and if you'd have told me it'd be a cop I'm considering reproducing with, I'd have punched you in the face for lying."

"I know the feeling," she mutters. "So, this is pretty serious, huh?"

I let out a long breath. "Yeah. It really is. I've never had something feel like this before."

"I've noticed a difference since you started dating him."

My eyes widen in surprise. "What kind of difference?"

"You're more confident. You don't seem as bothered by bull-shit. There's a spring in your step."

It's on the tip of my tongue to tell her that has nothing to do with Kyle and everything to do with killing pieces of shit. I'm doing my part to save the world, one woman-beating rapist at a time. That tends to give you some pep through your day. It's better than coffee, and I move through most of my day feeling like Batman. Part of my confidence is that I'm walking around with a million-dollar secret. That's power I've never known until now.

"Do you want it to be this serious?" Lucy asks, clasping her hands and focusing on me. It's unnerving.

I nod. "Yes. Very much so. I can't explain it," I say, my eyes darting around the room as I try to find words. "He just fits. *We* just fit. It's like searching the world for literally decades and finding someone with jagged pieces who fits *your* jagged pieces. It's like we were a glass that broke into two parts and found each other. I don't know how to describe it."

When I look up at Lucy, her eyes are wistful. "I understand more than you know. I mean, yeah, Aaron and I dated for years when we were young, but we weren't together very long as adults before we got engaged. When it's right, it's right. It's not like you met three days ago and are going to run off and get married tomorrow."

"That would be stupid, but I definitely see a future with him."

We sit in silence for another minute, and I tap my feet on the floor. There's an elephant in the room, and I'm rooted to the seat. Lucy wrings her hands and looks at her phone before I notice she turns the entire thing off. Without needing direction, I reach into my purse and also turn mine completely off.

"What does he know about Daniel?" she asks once both devices are powered down.

"Nothing. He knows he's missing, of course. You said that night that we'd never talk about it again, so I haven't brought it up with you. But do you think I'm in danger from Kyle?"

"I didn't want to talk about it again, but then you started dating a cop, of all fucking professions, a few months later. Not that I'm one to talk. Aaron says Kyle's nice enough but doesn't really get involved in drama or talk much. It's hard to get a read on him, but he's not overly ambitious. He probably isn't actively looking into it. He took your statement, right?"

I told her about Kyle calling me in for questioning, but that's as much as we've spoken about it. Lucy asked me if I sang like a canary or if I got a hint that they were on to her or Ellen, but I didn't get that from Kyle.

"Kyle hasn't mentioned anything about it. If the police suspected something amiss, certainly he'd bring it up, even in casual conversation."

"Does he ask about Daniel at all?"

"Nope." It's one of the things I like about him. He knows my past, and he's content to keep it firmly in the past.

Lucy inhales deeply. "What if he finds out?"

"He won't."

"What if he does? What is your plan? Hurt him?"

"Never!"

"Run?"

"Probably that, but he's a cop. He could probably find me anywhere. It's not like running away from a local drug dealer who doesn't want attention on themselves."

"You need a plan on what to do if he finds out."

I rub my temples and squeeze my eyes shut. "It's blowing over. It won't come to that."

The Daniel thing *is* blowing over. As far as I know, his parents have a private investigator still looking, but the police don't know anything. There's no body. No credit card trail. I'm thankful he must have used cash for gas on the way here or filled up before coming. I have no idea where his car is, and if the police have located it, I haven't heard. It wasn't in Lucy's lot or nearby. Lucy and I checked the roads and ditches on our way to the campground that night. He could have taken the bus or a plane, but there'd be some trail there. He never came to my house, and I can prove that. Doorbell cameras installed by the neighbors would catch his car coming up the street. The boys even vouched he hadn't been there when their grandparents called. They didn't lie because it was the truth. I've gone about life as normal because there's nothing that connects me to his disappearance.

"It'll be fine," I say, doing my best to comfort Lucy. She scowls and crosses her arms. "I know you don't believe me, but they'd need a body. I have motive as his frequent court petitioner, but they have nothing tangible tying me to him. In their eyes, I need my child support from him, so I may not be eager to see him dead. If they narrow it down to that night, I have an alibi because I was working here, for fuck's sake. I taught a class of women who will vouch that I was here. You'll say I was here. Will someone really think he showed up at your pole gym and started shit with me?"

"Probably not a smart idea."

"It wasn't! He got murdered because of it."

"Probably not murdered, per se. It's not like you did it on purpose."

"I liked it, though."

Lucy's entire posture changes from loose, like she's so tired she's trying to remain upright, to stiffening like a statue. "I'm sure it was gratifying in a revenge way."

That's putting it mildly. I liked it so much that I've been taking other dirtbags out of the gene pool.

She gets up from her desk and slings her purse over her shoulder. "I need to get home. I'm exhausted. Just...be careful, will you? You killed a man, whether it was murder or not. Now you're involved with a cop. Don't tell him anything just because you love him and want to get it off your chest. If you ever feel bad about it and need to vent, you vent to me."

I stand and also grab my things. "Are you worried I'll say something to get you in trouble?" I ask.

"Honey, I'm worried we're all going down for this."

All? Does she mean Aaron? Why would Aaron go down for anything? Surely she means Ellen who let us use her campground to burn and then ditch what was left into the pond. I should have done that with Jake's body, but I wasn't sure if I had time. I wrongly thought the fire was enough.

"I don't think Kyle knows anything or suspects anything."

There's no way he could make love to me like he has if I was a killer. Most people would go screaming in the other direction. I don't think he'd turn me in, but he sure wouldn't date me. Someone would have to be certifiably crazy to do that.

"Promise me, no matter what, that you'll skip town if the shit hits the fan," Lucy says. "Don't stay and point fingers. I have a family I'm worried about, and you should be worried about your boys."

"I am."

It's not a lie. It's why I don't kill every week. I'm sure as shit going to let the current media shitstorms settle down before I take out anyone else.

Chapter 20

Kyle

There was no good way to do this. Believe me, I spent three nights awake, one of them with Cheryl right next to me, and it's still consumed my thoughts. I'm surviving on caffeine and seriously considering something harder at this point, but I've wracked my brain and made three pros and cons lists.

How do you tell the woman you love that you're on to her? How do you hide what she did to everyone else on the planet but somehow make it known to her that she's in danger of getting caught?

I covered for her, of course. Everyone would hide the evidence if it meant that a woman they love would go to jail for life and leave behind a good relationship and two boys who need her. Sure, she should have thought about the boys before she started lighting people on fire, but hindsight is twenty-twenty.

I scrubbed the tape. I was alone in the review room, and I did a little looping. I even did a little magic with AI and loaded it over the top, making the tape show Portsmith walking out of screen range right as rain and definitely alive. If Angela saw him get picked up by a mystery woman, we can't see it. All we have to go on is Angela's testimony that it happened.

No woman on the camera means no warrant for Cheryl.

Cheryl needs to stop, though. She's new at this and will get caught eventually. All it would have taken to get caught this time is for Coleson to have been in the room. She's lucky it was me. At the end of the day, there's no Hallmark card that says, "Hey, I know you're a killer, but I love you and think I want to marry you."

I've thought about a simple, anonymous letter. I've also thought about just knocking on her door and telling her. I know she would never hurt me. People would probably think I'm crazy for saying she's safe for me, but she wouldn't and couldn't hurt me.

I'm not *most people*. When people say there's a lid for every pot, they're talking out me and Cheryl.

At present, I sit across the street from her house in a plain car I borrowed from the motor pool. It's one we use on stakeouts, or it's loaned out for the odd undercover work. I'm just another basic car parked on an average street in front of a neighbor's house.

I duck down in the seat and wait for her to come home. I watch the boys walk home from the bus stop, and I hold my breath as they walk past the mailbox. I wait for half an hour as the boys go inside, probably to eat an after-school snack, and then come out to toss a football around. I make a mental note to buy them a new one or teach them to inflate the one they have. I can see it partially deflated from here. Maybe they don't have a pump. Damn, I like those kids. Never, in a million years, would I have thought I'd love and accept another man's kids. They may look like their dickbag father, but I see so much of Cheryl in their personalities. Strong. Intelligent. Somehow, loving *her* has made me care about *them*.

Fuck, I hope they're not home when their mom checks the mail.

I let out a deep sigh when I see Lenore waddle across the street and speak to Jonah for a few seconds before the boys nod and walk off with her. Perfect. I hope they'll stay over there. Cheryl mentioned that they sometimes stay with Lenore on Friday nights to stay up late playing video games. The boys often eat dinner with the woman, and I hope that's the case now so Mom can crash out when she opens the yellow envelope. More than once, they've fallen asleep over at Lenore's on a weekend while playing *Rocket League*, and I hope tonight is one of those nights.

Ten minutes later, Cheryl's car rolls into the driveway and my breath hitches. My heart pounds so hard I check my pulse, worried I'm having a heart attack. I pull up the collar of my shirt because I worry she'll look over at the cross street and find me watching her.

She must have been out running errands because she's wearing simple black leggings and an off-the-shoulder sweatshirt that looks retro. No club wear for the strip club or Lucy's workout place. Her pink bra strap on her shoulder catches my eye, and it almost makes me get out, walk across the street, and cover it so no man looking out of his window can see her underthings.

That's a pretty intense thought for a man who's in love with a stripper. Men see way more of her than her bra. I cock my head and think about that a moment while I watch her open her trunk and grab a small plastic bag containing what looks like a grocery store rotisserie chicken. Why doesn't it bother me that she strips? Most guys would have a problem with their girl taking off their clothes for money, right? Is it because I love her? Trust that she won't do anything with another man? When did I get so trusting of monogamy? It's an odd feeling that I've not really had before in other relationships. Call it an occupational hazard, but I don't usually trust anyone or anything.

I trust her.

I hold my breath as she walks to the mailbox and pulls out the utility bills I laid back on top of the envelope when I pushed the packet inside. I know one is her water bill and another is the gas. One is a bill from the hospital, probably for her son's arm a few weeks back. I pat my wallet in my front pocket, mostly subconsciously, as I think about helping her with that bill. Lord fucking knows Daniel won't be able to help financially anymore, and medical bills are a cunt that's destroyed more than one single mother.

I watch the moment she tilts her head in curiosity, pulling the large envelope out of the mailbox. Maybe she has a sense of foreboding because she looks left and right up the street. Thankfully, she doesn't look in my direction, not that she'd really see me. It's still daylight, and she probably couldn't see me at this range, even if I wasn't stuffed down in my seat. She looks at Lenore's house, possibly wondering if the old woman found the random twenties and threw them in an envelope to send right back to her.

I lean forward in my seat and watch as she opens the mailer. Has she noticed there's no return address?

When she slides the screenshot I took of her and Portsmith talking on the sidewalk out of the envelope, I watch her mouth open in an O. Her eyes widen in fear. It wasn't my intention to scare her catatonic. I just wanted to put a bit of fear into her, enough to make her stop. She doesn't know what she's doing. She's not a professional. She's doing this hastily, even I can see that. It's sloppy, and if Avery ever gets a print, it's game over.

There's also a thumb drive containing the original video in the envelope, and Cheryl pulls it out, staring at it as she turns it in the sunlight like she's studying a diamond's authenticity. A moment later, she shoves it and the picture back into the envelope, looks up and down the street again, and then turns the envelope over, probably hunting for a return address, postmark, or any clue as to who sent this to her.

Cheryl walks to her porch, fumbles with her keys, gives up when she can't get the key in the hole because her hands are shaking, and crumples onto the concrete as soon as she's out of sight from most of her neighbors. She pulls her hair as she opens her mouth again in a silent scream.

My legs itch to move. I should hold her. Comfort her. Instead, my fingers turn the key in the ignition, and I pull my seatbelt on, back into the driveway a few yards behind me, and speed away in the other direction. I should have just told her directly instead of using a fucking envelope. I thought it would be best, but the anonymous nature of sending her pictures has obviously done more harm than good.

I fucked that up, and we're due a conversation.

I'll come back. Tonight. We need to have a long talk and get some things straight. Hopefully, the boys are at Lenore's for the evening and I can comfort her. Like a frustrated parent, I'm just going to give Cheryl Briggs a few hours to go to her room and think about what she's done.

CHAPTER 21

Cheryl

Two panic attacks. New world record. Thankfully, the boys aren't home, and a quick phone call to Lenore will keep them firmly over there for the night. No use scaring them as I shove things into a black trash bag, only to take the items out later.

I should move. Take the boys and run far away.

I should stay and see what happens. The boys have school and running could mean that someone thinks I'm guilty of making Daniel go missing. I mean, I did make Daniel go missing, but that's not the point.

I should leave and tell the boys and anyone who asks that I just needed a change of scenery. Maybe I can send a card to Daniel's parents telling them where I am if Daniel needs to contact me. That would throw them off, right?

A banging sound interrupts my third packing of the trash bag, and my heart stops in my chest before I smack my ribcage like I'm forcing the organ to work again. That sounded like a police knock. Should I turn off the lights? That'd be obvious. Pretend I'm not home?

I stand still and stare at the door without blinking, my heart now pounding in my ears and showing me I'm definitely alive. Fucked, but alive.

"Cheryl, baby, I know you're in there. Open the door."

Kyle.

I look around my living room and cringe at the sight of the boys' clothes spread out on the coffee table, having been removed from the trash bag and left there. I drop the bag to the floor, smooth my hair, and slowly walk to the door. Just as I reach it, Kyle bangs on it again, making me jump.

"Just a second." My voice is weak and trembling. Fuck, I hope he doesn't know about Jake Portsmith.

When I open the door, Kyle's in street clothes. Something about seeing him out of uniform makes my eyes flutter in relief. If he came to arrest me, he'd be in uniform. Dwyer would be standing behind him with a warrant to search my house, a look of disappointment on his face. There'd be other men and women in uniform here, guns on their hips. Kyle's wearing jeans and a soft, gray T-shirt that I know from experience smells like a hint of citrus. No weapon at his waistband. Just...Kyle. I look behind him one more time and then wave him into the house, shutting and locking the door like I expect the SWAT team after him.

He looks around my living room, and his brow furrows at the trash bag on the floor. "Packing?"

"No," I lie. "Just, uh, going through the boys' things to see what fits. I may sell some lots of clothes on eBay or Facebook Marketplace to get a few extra bucks." I paste a fake smile on my face. "How are you?" I try not to cringe when I draw out the words. Great. He knows I'm lying or up to something.

He gives a cursory glance around the room again and then focuses on me. There's something different about his eyes now, though. Something dark, like a shadow moving over his face. His lips draw into a thin line and he backs against the entry to the kitchen, propping his elbow against the door frame. "Sweetheart, is there anything you want to tell me?"

There's so much I want to tell him. But it's a lot, and I'd need a *Cliff's Notes* version to give him all the information before dawn. That's how long it would take to tell him about Daniel, about me being a teen, about the abuse, and the fear. It would take me hours to tell him about how I found my victims and how I researched their sins. How I decided how to kill them. All of it jumbles in my brain as he stands there and stares at me. My eyes flick to the envelope still on top of the kitchen table, and my watery eyes move back to find his head tilted and a snarky grin on his face.

Just then, the grin gets bigger and he slowly looks over his shoulder at the envelope on the table and then back at me. "I'll ask again. Is there something you want to tell me?"

"No."

"I know, Cheryl. I sent the envelope, hoping you'd stop now." He holds up a hand as I open my mouth to deny everything. "Don't worry, it's just for us. Not one other soul will see it, but you need to stop."

I take two steps away from him, shaking my head as the rest of my body trembles. He knows! I'm going to lose him. My brain whirls. I should come clean. No, I should deny, deny, deny. But this is Kyle. I should admit it. No, I should tell him he doesn't know what he's talking about. Certainly, I can come up with some kind of explanation of why there's a picture of me on the street with Jake Portsmith.

"I don't know what you're talking about," I say, desperate to say something.

"Baby, I think you do," he coos. His voice is different.

I shake my head as my face heats. "I don't understand," I whisper.

"Oh, I understand you very well." He pushes off the door frame but doesn't approach me. Doesn't close the space between us. "I want to help you. Help you stop. You're going to get caught because you're sloppy and inexperienced, and the only reason you're not in a jail cell right now is because I erased any proof and fixed the CCTV video from Dryden's. You were blessed by simple police scheduling. It was me who watched the tape, not Coleson. Not Dwyer. Not another deputy."

I shake my head more. My mouth opens in wracking sobs. "I'm sorry."

He smiles again like this is a fun game.

Wait. What?

"Sweetheart, don't apologize to me. I get it. I know why you killed Jake Portsmith. Just like I know why you killed Daniel and Troy Acox."

The room spins like I'm drunk. My legs buckle, and this time he steps forward and catches me, gently gripping my elbow as he helps me back to my feet.

I whine, "No!" at the same time he says, "There, there."

He presses both hands to my shoulders and then lets go, raising his index finger to his smirk and making a shush sign.

"I don't understand."

"I know everything, and I've suspected a lot since before I even saw that footage. Well, suspected about Acox. I'm not going to lie, I kind of suspected about Portsmith before the tape. We found an ATM receipt from the club in his house, and Acox's friends mentioned the last time they saw him was at the club. It was too much of a coincidence. I *knew* about Daniel."

I shake my head like I'm clearing cobwebs. "How did you know I killed Daniel?"

He leans in close, so close that I'm tempted to kiss him. Wait. Is he going to kiss me after finding out I've been murdering people? Then again, he's known for more than just a few minutes unless he's making shit up. We fucked two nights ago.

"I've always known what you are since you sat in that chair at the station and nervously crossed your legs. It's why I was so attracted to you. I've always known you killed the boys' father. You were so nervous at the police interview. I suspected you were doing other naughty things unbefitting a lady, but I didn't have total proof until the Portsmith video."

"How long have you known about Jake?"

"Definitively? A few days."

A gasp escapes my throat before I can stop it. "Why didn't you say anything the other night?"

He idly strokes my chin and then runs his finger down my neck. "Because I found out an interesting tidbit about myself. I like fucking a killer. It caters to my...masochistic side." He tilts his head from side to side. "And I'm a little in love. Right from the very beginning. I didn't know how to tell you I knew. I made so many lists with pros and cons, baby."

"You found me interesting because I'm killing men?"

"I was fascinated with a woman taking vigilante justice into her own hands. You don't see enough of that these days. Rapists get away with it. Assaults are swept under the rug. I get it." He pauses and places a soft kiss on my forehead. "My soul mate."

I shake my head like he slapped me instead of kissing my forehead, even though I know Kyle Mitchell would never strike me. He's not Daniel. "Your soul mate? Because you're a police officer and I'm a killer? Yin and Yang? We both seek justice?"

The air tightens in the room after the last words of my question leave my mouth. It's the feeling before something big happens. It's after the bomb goes off but before the blast torches everything. It's the rumble before loud thunder. I reflexively shrink, expecting it.

"No," he says in a low, husky voice. He runs his finger up my cheek, and his eyes follow the movement. "I was on to you since you nervously crossed your legs at the station about Daniel because there's something dark inside you that we recognize in those of us who also have it. But it was only when I found the tape of you and Portsmith that I realized you have a taste for it and killed the others."

"I don't understand."

"One of the men wasn't yours that you killed, right?"

Heat floods my cheeks, and my veins heat as my heart pumps faster. "Someone is like me and they're copying me." I gulp.

He nods. "There's someone like you, actually a couple people I can think of, but they're not copying you."

"What do you mean?"

"They're protecting you."

Cold dread moves into my stomach. I reach for him and flex my fingers into the fabric on his chest. He pulls me close and kisses my cheek before settling his jaw against mine.

"I never killed Mark Ricord, Kyle," I whisper next to his face, his skin hot against mine. "I swear to fucking God."

Kyle runs his finger across my cheek again, this time down my face. He pulls back a bit, frowns, and the spot between his eyebrows creases again.

"I know, sweetheart. I believe you," he whispers. "I know you didn't do it because I chopped his dick off and skinned that mother fucker alive *for* you."

Chapter 22

Cheryl

The world spins against its normal rotation. I momentarily can't hear anything as blood pounds in my ears. Tears run down my cheeks on both sides of my face, and I'm sure my mascara is going with it. My heart pounds like knocking against my rib cage, and I take jagged breaths as I wrap my head around what he just said. His words are like a punch to the chest when your lungs contract and you gasp for air, only to not find any.

Kyle?

Kyle killed Mark Ricord?

He backs away from me, probably to give me space, and braces the door frame with one hand, leaning against it nonchalantly like he owns the place. Hell, if we stay together, he probably will someday, or we'd give it up if I move in with him. I shake my head. I can't believe I'm thinking about living arrangements right now. Should I break up with him? Run? Hide? My mind spins.

My sons.

I don't think he'd hurt them, but I also don't think he'd hurt me. He killed for me. He tortured for me. He skinned a man and strung him up like a deer. Or strung him up and skinned him after cutting body parts off. I squeeze my eyes shut and try not to think about the order he did it.

Something about all this goes way beyond revenge killing, but I can't focus. My mind searches like it's looking for the right key for a lock. None of this makes sense. *I'm* the killer. Me! Kyle's the innocent lawman. I should be hiding from him, not listening as he brazenly tells me he killed an elected official.

He clucks at me and shakes his head. "Baby, come on!" he yells, very out of character for him. Then, he chuckles. "You're my world now, and I'd burn it down for you, but if you think I've only killed once and need to copy anything you do, you're selling me short." He places his hand on his chest. "I'm actually kind of offended. I can be a prideful bastard about my work."

A laugh bubbles from my chest, but I swallow it down. Fuck, this is what he meant by us being soul mates.

Oh. My. Fucking. God. Ricord wasn't a one-and-done? Kyle Mitchell is a serial killer, and he's been flying under the radar. But for how long?

So much suddenly makes sense. I suddenly understand his aversion to telling me why he left Buffalo. I remember Lucy telling me that Aaron thinks Kyle is quiet and not ambitious.

He's been that way to fly under the radar. He's more observant than the average police officer. I should have known when he stiffened after I mentioned Ricord a few days ago and then covered up the emotion. I was too worried he was on to me to ever think he had something to do with it.

Kyle Mitchell is a master of masking.

"How many?" I ask, practically choking the words out.

He shrugs and looks at my ceiling. He could be thinking, counting in his head, or even just investigating the ceiling for water spots. None of this ruffles him.

"Are we going to compare body counts now? Literal body counts, that is? Funny that most dating couples compare very different body counts. But I'll play along. Let's see..." His voice trails off as he rubs his chin and looks at my ceiling. "Eighteen. Maybe Nineteen." He waffles his head from side to side as my eyes widen so much that I worry they'll pop out of their sockets. "People like us, we lose track over time, right?" he asks with a chuckle.

"I don't."

"How very moral of you. I'll let you have this one, and we'll chalk you up as the better person."

"I'm having some trouble understanding what you're saying." I grit my teeth. "Tell me what you are."

"The same thing you are, Cheryl." He smiles to himself and looks at the ceiling again. A small hum comes from his throat. "Don't you feel close to me? Don't I feel like home to you the way you do to me? Haven't you been able to explain why that is? I'm the same type of creature we seem to be experiencing in this county over the last year. There's another one of us here, if you didn't already know. They haven't killed lately, but that could be because of..." His voice trails off again, and he smiles a shit-eating grin like he knows something I don't. But I *do* know he's talking about Lucy. "Reasons," he continues. "But you and I are cut from the same cloth and here because of the same circumstances."

"How are we the same?"

He makes a swiping motion with his hand, batting my question away. "Do you know what it's like having to pretend I'm a bumbling idiot at work? A quiet mouse? Just a sweet, well-meaning guy? Because you know that's not the real me, right? It's a mask I wear to hide."

"I understand, Kyle. More than you'd ever know. I knew there was more to you when you named every brand I used from smell alone. If you think I don't know what it's like to be looked down on and underestimated, I can assure you that I do."

"Maybe that's why we're such a good fit," he says, coming closer so I can smell the gum in his mouth. He lifts my chin, using only his index finger again, and places a soft kiss on my lips. I can't help swooning a little and certainly can't help that my eyes flutter. I like it when he's in charge. I'm safe then.

A man killed for me because the victim called me trash and told me I shouldn't pay my taxes late. Is there ever a more intense way of showing someone you love them?

He rubs his nose against mine, a move so playful I relax my shoulders. "This is my second department," he whispers. "You asked on our first date why I left Buffalo. I had to leave because some bad guys just kind of... disappeared, you know? People started to sniff around since I was in on the cases. I was a reporting officer at domestic disputes on two of them. Two of the guys beat their wives so badly that the women needed plastic surgery. I was a connection, so I left. I moved here and got a job being the lovable and bumbling deputy who could see a lot more than I let on, but I never solved the cases I worked. I let Coleson or Dwyer take the credit, or I pointed them to something that seemed like I accidentally found it. Nobody suspects you if you're smart enough to tie your shoes but bumbling enough to not be taken too seriously. Sure, I can push pieces together or raise my hand to ask a good question that sparks an idea in management every now and then, but I see more than people think I do. I saw you."

"You knew and slept with me anyway?"

"Baby, I love fucking you, but this is more than sex. You and I both know it. I love you," he says, swiping his finger down my nose and then booping the tip. "You made a valiant effort to hide things well. I'm impressed. Kind of proud, really."

"Why do you kill?" I ask in a whisper. "I kill because I'm angry and men hurting people makes me even more pissed off. I don't hurt anyone innocent."

"I know." He nods. "I don't blame you, and you'll never hear me taunt you with that. At some point, your compassion broke. Maybe it was when Daniel showed up, but something took you from angry bitch to enraged cunt. I understand because I'm angry, too. It's why I kill. What's the old saying? Hurt people hurt people? Something like that. I'm like you, though. I don't kill the innocent. I don't even hurt people who piss me off with little things. I don't kill phone scammers or the poor people who steal from the gas station because their families need food. I only kill the disgustingly guilty who hurt everyday people and enjoy it. I only kill men who hurt women, children, and even other men they see as beneath them. I enjoy hurting them. It..." He gestures to the top of his stomach and rubs his hand over the area. "It feeds me. It takes away the pain in ways other things can't."

He closes his eyes and inhales, letting the breath out a second later. Does he also breathe in crisp, clean air when he kills? I make a note to ask him what it feels like for him someday. Does he feel powerful instead of powerless when he does it?

"It's why I can remain so calm and be so good at my job," he says, and I'm reminded of how calm he was in the club when Ricord was nose-to-nose with him. "It's because the real shitheads will get their due. Eventually. Slowly. Painfully. I can't react when I have the shield on my chest and the city uniform on, but I can do it on my day off."

My hands shake, so I shove them into my pocket. My heart pounds so loud I wonder if he can hear it. "Tell me why," I whisper. "What pushed you to enraged and vicious?"

"I've never told anyone."

It's too much, and my face crumbles at the thought of someone hurting him. Someone hurt him badly. I hear it in his voice. That's why he says we're just alike. The anger that moves up my body is crushing, and I can't help but reach out and run my hands up his chest, flexing my fingers over his pectoral muscles as I go.

"Do you really love me?" I ask.

"More than I can ever express to you or even physically show you, even if I fuck you every night for the rest of our criminally insane lives."

"Then tell me. If we're going to be in this shit together, I need to know, Kyle."

His eyes shut at my touch. He trusts me. "Are you asking for my villain origin story?"

"You know mine. Are we really villains, though, Kyle? Or are we the good guys after all?"

"I like to think I'm an antihero. I serve justice even when it's denied by the justice system. I do what I do to fight for the kids like me who couldn't fight. I fight for the women who are beaten down by small men. I'm no hero, though."

"What happened?" I ask again, whispering and running my hand up his forearm. He trembles at my touch. "You're safe with me. We're safe with each other."

His eyes dart around the room like he's weighing the benefits of telling me. After about ten seconds, he takes a deep breath, letting it out slowly a second later. "The guys were from school. You know the type," he whispers and then clears his throat to speak clearly. "The popular guys. We were all just fourteen and fifteen. I don't know why they picked me. I never harmed them and always kept to myself."

I move a lock of his hair that's fallen over his forehead. "It's OK. Did they do something? It wasn't your fault if they did."

"They lead me to the grownups that did. I guess some older men had something on them. Maybe the older men were relatives or giving them money or drugs. Maybe they were scared physically. The other kids' job was to bring weak little wimps like me to them. They looked for kids who could be held down and wouldn't be likely to talk to friends. I was probably picked because I didn't have many friends to tell. They asked me to a sleepover, and I thought I was so cool that they were including me. I felt special because I was the kid who couldn't even make the basketball team and hadn't grown an inch for years." He closes his eyes and takes another deep breath. I rub circles on his chest, letting him know I'm here. "I showed up, and we went on a hike in the woods. They talked it up as being a nature hike with flashlight tag and we even took one kid's parents' beer. The older men were in the woods waiting and..." He trails off.

My legs shake as my imagination spins back to my own prom and Daniel. "It's OK," I whisper, trying to hold it together for Kyle. "I've been there." And I have. I know the shame.

"The other kids got an envelope from one of the men and then took off, leaving me there while the older men pinned me down. There were three of them. All of these sick fucks were in their fifties or sixties. Please don't make me say the rest. I can't. Not even with you. It took me a long time to face myself in the mirror and put the pieces together of what happened." He takes a breath and closes his eyes. "I came home with a ripped shirt and sticks in my hair. No major marks except some bruising from fighting as best I could. My mom banged on the bathroom door for fifteen minutes asking why I was home and asking if something happened." He wipes a tear away from his cheek. "I wanted to tell her so fucking bad. I wanted to fall into her and cry, but if I had told my parents, it would have killed them simply because my mother would have never let it go until justice was served. I couldn't think. I couldn't do anything but hurt." He rolls his shoulders. "I felt so alone."

My heart pounds, and tears prick my eyelids. My hands shake and my bottom lip trembles with rage for the man I love. He looks down, not even able to meet my eyes.

"Just tell me one thing," I say. He presses his head against my forehead and shakes it like he can't handle much more sharing, and another tear leaks out of his eye, falling straight to my floor. I smile a maniacal grin, one only reserved for the likes of Troy Acox. "Did you make those sick assholes pay?"

He laughs at my question, and my stomach does a funny swoop. Something about the depravity in that smile. This man would protect me, but there's an evil streak. Not black or white. Gray. Kyle Mitchell is morally gray, and my heart pounds out of my chest at the sheer excitement of him not being the sweet police officer that I thought he was. Here I thought he was a rule follower all along, but he's so much more. I know, without a doubt, I'll never have to worry about someone hurting me or the boys ever again. I know it deep in my bones now. I can feel it in the set of his shoulders and in the way his forehead leans against mine. I'm his. He's mine. It's visceral. We're bound by our respective batshittery for eternity. Did the universe push us together?

I think back to the day of Lucy's wedding and how Kyle and I stared at each other. Did we see it in each other then? Unblinking love and adoration? Like the other half of your soul is suddenly found in a church pew? I must have seen my own damage and angst reflected back like I was looking into a mirror.

This is all as unhealthy as fuck, but God damn me to hell I love this man.

"I waited until I was nineteen," he says. "Until I was stronger and had experienced a growth spurt or two. I waited until they wouldn't see me coming. Then I picked the old men off one by one. One I made disappear. I took my time with him. He was so scared, but I don't know if he could ever be as scared as I was as a fourteen-year-old boy. I reminded him of that as I taunted him and tortured him until he begged me to slit his fucking throat at the end. I happily obliged. He was my first kill, and I wanted more. I think you know the feeling. I made the second man look like an accident. They were older, after all. I held the third down in his bathtub and slit his wrists, making it look like a suicide. I held him by his chin so hard his mouth was open and made him look at my face the whole time while the fucker bled out. I remember telling them all they fucked up one thing. They should have killed me that night."

"What about the teens?" I ask. "Did you get the guys that sold you out?"

"I waited a couple of years after the older men. I wanted them to wonder when they saw the deaths in the paper. Were they more relieved or did they worry? They would be harder to kill because they were my age and strong. I lifted. I got in shape before I even attempted to fuck with them in case they fought."

I roll my forehead against his, grinding into him. I'd melt into him if I could. "Is it bad that I'm really not able to live with the suspense, Kyle? I need to know what happened next."

He kisses my cheek and rests his jaw against mine again so that his breath hits my ear. "I love that you want justice for me, Cheryl, and I want justice for you. Maybe it's enough to keep us going in the coming years."

He wipes hair back from my face, and I lean into his hand.

"I got two of them," he says, finally answering my question. "Separate years. All on the night before Thanksgiving when everyone goes home and out to the bars. Roofied them and followed them out of the bar. One strangled. One with a knife. I dumped or got rid of them all in different ways. The first, I took to a local hog farm in the dead of night. The other is chopped up in bags and at the trash facility, probably already buried by years of dog shit bags and kitchen trash."

"The third?"

"Alive. I'll get him eventually. He was the ringleader. I want him scared and afraid to even move on in life and have a family. There's a vacation for us in our future if you're OK with spending a week in Buffalo."

"Don't you think that's a loose end?"

"No bodies. No proof. The older guy deaths were explained, and I never kill the same way twice. If you kill the same way or hide the bodies the same, the police think it's the same person. It's ideal to make it look random. What's the last guy going to do? Point a finger at a cop and tell them he sold my body to old men sixteen years ago and he's scared I'll seek revenge when the police in the area don't even have any idea they have a serial killer? They have a couple of missing white males, but no bodies, and I was careful."

My arms are around him in moments, and I hold onto him for dear life. His ribs expand with his breath, but the heat from him as he wraps his own arms around me moves through my body.

I love him. If the men that hurt him were still alive, I'd kill them myself.

Something else stirs in me, though.

Lust.

Want.

And I know he feels it too because his dick hardens against my stomach. That cock I know so well. The dick I've stroked, sucked, and fucked that knows exactly what I feel like inside. Is it sick that I want him more now that I know what he's capable of to protect the woman he loves?

Before I can think about it more, my hands are above my head as Kyle backs me against the wall, pinning me. He nuzzles my neck with his nose, bending a little. "Are you scared, Cheryl? Do you think I'll hurt you?"

His heaving chest presses against my breasts. I should be scared. Most normal women would be. But my nipples come to attention, mostly because I've never been normal. My body obviously didn't get the memo about Kyle Mitchell's dark side. If anything, they're still operating under the assumption that he'll flick his tongue over my tits and move south.

"I will never hurt you," he says. "Ever. Understand?"

Kyle's pupils dilate, and he shifts to holding my hands above my head with one hand. He pins me against the wall and grinds his hips into me. Before I can be sure if he's playing, erect, or just holding me against the wall, he pulls something from his pants. My breath hitches, and my stomach drops.

No.

He won't. He can't. He just said he would never hurt me. For the first time since I met him, I want to run from him. But I can't with his hands holding me in place and his hips pinning me against the wall.

Squeezing my eyes together, I clench my fists until my nails dig into my palms. This is a dream. A bad nightmare. I'll wake up if I scratch or pinch myself.

He notices my fear. "Oh, you think this is for you? Well, it's not."

My lip trembles, even with his comforting words.

"Hurt me," he whispers in my ear, pulling me out of my fear. The soft sound of the knife retracting fills the room.

"Wh-what?"

He smiles against my cheek and presses a warm kiss to my earlobe. "I like the pain. You know those scars I told you were from police work?"

"Yeah."

"I did that to myself."

I scowl at him as I piece it together. All the little scars over his thighs and arms, not to mention the tiny scars near where his legs meet his pelvis. "You're a masochist?" I whisper, drawing out the words. How did I not see it?

"It takes the pain away and helps me feel something besides what I feel when I think about what was done to me when I was just a teen. It helps me focus my shame and my anger and forget about it while I think about the present."

He presses the hilt of the small knife into my palm. The handle is warm from being in his pocket, and it takes me a second to realize what he wants me to do. Slowly, he lets go of me and grips the hem of his shirt, pulling it over his head. When the shirt is in a wrinkled jumble on my floor, he squares his shoulders and smiles, probably showing me the same grin his victims see in their last seconds.

He lifts his index finger and swipes it across his shoulder. "Right here, baby."

"I won't hurt you. I'd never hurt a good man. You've been nothing good to me. Good to my boys."

He brings his middle finger to his mouth and runs his tongue over the tip as he stares into my eyes. Fuck, he looks deranged when he licks his middle finger like that. I'm so screwed in the head for even thinking about how sexy he is when he begs and smirks like the world's biggest mother fucker.

When his finger is wet enough for his liking, he drags it to the side of his abdominals. "Or right here. It's OK. I want you to try it. I want you to feel what it's like sinking a blade into me. I'm curious if it feels different when the person is someone you love."

"I love you too much to hurt you," I sob. I shake my head. Not him. Not Kyle. "I don't hurt innocents!"

"Good thing I'm not innocent then, huh? I want you to hurt me to show me you love me." He bares his teeth. "I know you don't understand, but I'm begging you to make me hurt. Show me you'll take the pain away from me. I want it. It'll be the last thing, short of putting a ring on your finger, to bind me to you. Make no mistake, I plan on doing that, too."

His face crumples when I stay frozen, pleading. "I'm the only one who's ever cut my skin. I want you to be the only other person to touch me like that. You're allowed to cut me, Cheryl. You can cut me right down to my fucking core if you want."

A whimper comes from my chest, and Kyle brings his hand to my throat. His grip is tight but not so tight I can't breathe while he grinds his cock into my slit. "See, I'm hard at the idea of just you dragging that blade across my skin. Do it!" he commands.

Slowly, I touch the tip of the knife against his skin and whisper the blade across his left pectoral. He hisses as an inch of blood appears in a thin line.

"Happy now?" I ask. I try to drop the knife, but my fingers won't work. They're locked around the hilt.

He pushes me back against the wall. "You can do better than that. I've seen your handiwork with the piano wire. Bravo, by the way. You're not shy, so don't act fucking shy. Cut me!" He yells the last part. Spit flies out of his mouth and lands on my collarbone.

Before I can think better of it, my hand flies across his skin. I squeeze my eyes shut as I do it. For some reason, I can burn a mother fucker alive, but I can't watch the blood form on Kyle's skin.

He notices and fists my hair, forcing my face up to him. "Look at me. Let me see those beautiful eyes while you hurt me. It feels so fucking good. Don't worry. I love this." He hums in approval. "Again."

I shake my head, and he pulls my hair a little harder. Not enough to hurt me. It's just enough to show me who's boss, and he's definitely the boss here. I *want* him to be in charge of us physically.

I do what he says again and whisper the blade over his other pectoral, this time opening one eye while I'm doing it. Kyle throws his head back as the blade cuts through him, and the look on his face is the same one he has when he comes. His eyes close in utter fucking rapture, and his shoulders visibly relax. As the blade opens his skin, a sound like a purr comes from his throat. He looks back down at me with hazy, unfocused eyes. I'll never understand masochism fully, but he's out of his head now. There's nothing but dark pits where his eyes once were.

The look on his face shows me this is either going to be very bad or very fucking good.

He lifts me with both hands under my ass and spins toward my room before I can wrap my head around the action. His blood leaks through my shirt, and the hot liquid heats my stomach. A metallic smell fills my nostrils, and I take deep breaths as that scent mixes with the usual citrusy man scent that's just Kyle. My mind spins with connecting the dots that this is Kyle, my sweet Kyle, but also...not Kyle.

He kicks my door closed but then turns and locks it, probably worried the boys will come home. The gesture makes my heart clench. He cares about the boys, but he loves me. He's willing to take my crazy if I take his, and he's willing to take the boys along with it.

He walks me gently to the bed, and I quickly kick off my pants and underwear and watch as Kyle drags his finger over the cut across his chest that's already clotting. Looking at me, he kneels between my legs and sucks the blood off his finger.

"Mmm," he practically purrs before gathering more blood on his fingertip and holding it out for me. "Want a taste?"

I open my mouth like a baby bird, and Kyle gently presses his bloody finger against my waiting tongue. The taste of iron fills my mouth, and I hum as a small droplet trickles down the back of my throat. When he drags his finger away, I sit up and attack the cut on his chest like a starving vampire, sucking and flicking my tongue over the wound as his fingers twine in my hair. Warm liquid fills my mouth, and I marvel that the taste is similar to cum. Both of Kyle's fluids are salty with a twinge of something savory.

"That's it. Drink me down. All of me. *Consume* me, baby. Take every drop of me if it makes you happy. This is all I've wanted since the day you walked away from me at the police station. I'd be lying if I said I haven't thought of you doing this when I cut."

His blood pools at the corners of my mouth, and I lick it away, only to return to the wound on his chest. He cradles my head as I take long pulls off it, and I look up at him with doe eyes like I do when I blow him. When he starts to clot and the blood slows, he guides the knife in my hand across another spot on his other pectoral. This time, I don't drink from him. I just watch the slow line drip from his body and onto my hips, ultimately dribbling to my sheets.

Kyle's shoulders heave as he controls himself from outright attacking me. I see the restraint in his eyes, the way he doesn't blink.

He moves my hand and makes another slit at his side where his ribcage meets his armpit. "One more," he whispers, closing his eyes and smiling a wry grin. "You can always cut me here. It's a spot rarely seen because my arm covers it. It's one of my favorite spots."

I want to say I'll never cut him again, but it's a lie. I can't make the promise that this will be a one-time thing. Whatever he asks me to do, I'll do it. He's asked me to stop murdering, so I'll stop. He's asked me to make him bleed, and I've done it. I know, somewhere in the dark recesses of my brain, that I'll do it again if that's what he needs.

The cut at his side bleeds profusely as he runs his palm over it and collects the blood in his hand. I quickly undo his pants, pull his dick from his underwear, and watch with wide eyes as he fists his cock, smearing the blood over it before running his fingers from my clit to my pussy. "Are you wet for me?"

"So fucking wet, Kyle," I whisper.

Fuck me, but I'm soaking at the sight of the man I love on his knees between my legs and his blood dribbling down his cock like we're on the set of a horror film. If I thought I was crazy before, I know now that I'm downright certifiable because I'm hot at the idea of Kyle also putting his blood on my slit and licking it off.

God damn me straight to hell because that's exactly what he does. He drags his finger up my slit one more time, sticks his fucking finger in his mouth, and then wipes another line of blood off his chest before bringing his hand back to my core.

He moves down my body so fast that it takes me a moment to spread my legs wider for his face. He's like a thirsty man attacking a glass of water after days in the desert. There are no soft licks or tongue flicks I associate with Kyle eating my pussy on a normal day. His lips go for my clit and wrap around the throbbing nub, sucking and pulling until my head spins and I see stars when I squeeze my eyes shut.

"Kyle," I moan as he sucks and flicks at the same damn time. His hands grip my hips and hold me down. In the past, he gently explored my body as he feasted on me. This time, he has one goal of making me come as soon as possible.

He hums in approval against my clit before roughly pushing my legs wide and moving to my pussy where he hardens his tongue and thrusts inside of me three times. He moves back to my clit and sucks so hard that he comes off me with a wet sound.

It's when he drags his finger once more across his bleeding chest and slides it inside of me that I lose all control over my body and mind. I clench around his digit, and he sucks my clit harder, not urging me on with words. The only encouragement I get is the soft moans coming from Kyle's throat as I face fuck him. I buck against him as he plays with my G spot, and his mouth works magic on all the other good parts. I grip his hair, and he chuckles a sound that's downright maniacal.

Maybe it's the unhinged laugh. Or the finger. Or the mouth. Whatever it is, I break apart, shaking so hard I worry something is wrong with me. I rock against his face harder, and I'm pretty sure I scream bloody murder.

Ironic.

The room spins like I'm drunk, and I momentarily worry I'll pull Kyle's curls all out of his head as my fingers grapple against him, trying to find purchase of something. Anything. My thighs squeeze his head, but he licks and flicks through my pleasure, and he even groans, humping the bed under me and showing me he's desperate to fuck.

When I'm done shaking, he places a soft kiss on my clit and slides his finger from my pussy. I whimper, missing it. I think about begging for another round, but I don't miss the finger so much as being filled with one of his body parts. Somewhere, in the back of my mind, I sit with that thought for a second.

I hate being physically separated from this man.

He enters me in one movement, and I gasp, arching my back and opening my mouth in a silent scream as he thrusts at a relentless pace without waiting for my body to adjust like he's done in the past. One bloody hand is gently at my throat, holding me down. Next to me, his other bloody hand grips the pillow, his fingers flexing and unflexing in rhythm with his thrusts. A drop of his sweat drips from his brow and onto my cheek. Sweat. Blood. Cum. I have no idea which one is which. All I know is that I'm warm and full as Kyle fucks me at a hard pace, breathing heavily above me.

Moans and slight whimpers eke out of my chest every time Kyle goes balls deep into me no matter how much I try to bite my lip and be quiet.

Kyle does no such thing. This man fully lets go without any shame or concern for whether or not he exudes masculinity. It's the sexiest fucking thing I've ever seen or heard. He cusses, moans, and spews utter filth from his lips, the kind I've never heard, not even while working at a strip club. I reach up and roll the blood droplets over his chest, bloodying my own hands as I massage his pecs.

I've been fucked many times before but not like this. Kyle Mitchell *owns* me. He claims every part of my body, marking me as his without branding or another form of abuse. This is sharing. Plain and simple.

He rolls his neck and whines, finally letting go of the pillow and positioning himself on his knees. I stare down the length of him, blood and sweat mixed together all the way down to his cock sliding in and out of me. A watery pink mixture runs to where we meet. His eyes fixate on the spot as we both watch the drops land on my slit, his length sliding into my core. He grips my hips and leaves bloody handprints I wish I could tattoo there. Never, in all my adult life, have I ever felt so loved. So utterly possessed.

"Turn over for me," he directs in a gruff voice. Something about his voice is urgent, and I whine in frustration when I flip over and his cock slips out for a second. He gives a quiet chuckle. "Don't worry. It'll be back soon." He pulls my hair until I grunt and have to look at the ceiling from the way he holds it. "I don't plan on my dick being very far from you ever again, Cheryl."

I position myself on my hands and knees, give a silent apology to the state of my sheets, and brazenly stick my ass in the air for him, offering myself to him like a common whore.

He grips my hips again and enters me hard. When he moves, the sound of our bodies meeting almost makes me giggle. Any other time, I would. But not tonight. The sound is a sign of utter fucking power as he pistons into me, moaning and growling as he thrusts. Never has a man let go with me like this. Never has a man shown his vulnerability by showing me exactly what I do to him. His visceral power transfers to me because I can make this man, this absolute predator, lose his fucking mind.

His hands tremble against my skin, and I look over my shoulder at him. I watch as he squeezes his eyes shut. I watch as he rolls his neck in pleasure. I watch as he bites his lip even as his face relaxes as he chases his own orgasm. When he finally opens his eyes and catches my gaze, he leans forward without blinking and presses his forehead to mine, never missing a thrust.

With one hand, he reaches around to my clit, and I'm a goner.

"Kyle," I shriek as my body tenses and trembles around his cock, milking him relentlessly for what seems like a heavenly minute but is probably just seconds. He immediately follows me over the edge like he was waiting for me to have one more orgasm all along, saying my name this time like it's the most loved name in the world. The way he says it signals that, without a doubt, it's the only name he wants to say.

I fall onto the ruined sheets, and he falls onto my back. He sweeps my sweaty hair back from my face, and I close my eyes with the warm mattress at my front and the man I love at my back. I feel a light kiss on my jaw, and then he's quiet, possibly relaxing like he's been waiting his whole life to feel safe with someone and has finally found her.

He can sleep now. Rest.

"I love you," he whispers. "Forever. It's me and you. Is that what you want?"

"More than anything," I say before letting out a long breath I didn't know I'd been holding for twelve fucking years.

Somehow, we found each other in this fucked-up world, and I'm never letting him go.

EPILOGUE

Kyle

Dwyer sips his coffee and hangs up the phone before waving me into his office. His expression is light, a small smile on his face. It's a nice change to the grouchiness of late. I know he has a lot on his mind.

I hate ruining his day.

Some things must be asked, though. No use sweeping it under the rug another day, week, or month.

I check behind me to make sure his secretary isn't around and idly lay the paper I'm holding on his desk. I can hear Bertie on the phone with someone else well beyond the door. "Mind if I ask you a question, Boss?"

"Shoot," he grumbles, not even looking at me.

"It's about how you coped with something."

He finally looks up, frowns, and tilts his head, confused. "How did I cope with what, Mitchell?"

I lean over his desk, meet his eyes, and square my shoulders back. He's my boss, and I've always been a little afraid of him. He literally controls my pay. If he wants to fire me, he could destroy my whole career. He could ask questions about deaths in Buffalo and deaths here that may be a little too similar. Heat moves up my spine, but it's not with lust like it is when I'm with Cheryl.

It's with the balls to finally ask what's been on my mind for almost a year. I'm also here to form an alliance I never thought I'd have to form. No use dragging it out.

"How do you handle being married to a murderer like Lucy?"

I expected a reaction, but he's even faster than I thought he'd be. He's out of his chair and leaning over his desk with his hand on my throat in a split second. Papers flutter with his quick movement, and pens from his desk roll and hit the floor. His carefree demeanor that was there just a moment ago washes away from his eyes as I gasp with shock and my fingers scrabble against his hand to let go of me.

"What the fuck are you talking about?" Dwyer whispers, glaring. His lip curls in rage, and his face is beet red.

My vision tunnels. I just asked a question, but my boss legit may kill me right in this room. I didn't foresee that happening when I asked for girl advice. I won't give in, though. Aaron Dwyer and I need to team up to make sure none of us go down. This is a long time coming.

"I just..." My voice trails off as I try to catch my breath. I inhale through my nose, and Dwyer loosens his fingers enough for me to speak in a dry whisper. "I need advice."

A noise outside the office pulls Aaron out of his murderous rage, and he releases me so hard that I stumble back against the guest chair behind me. He walks to the door, opens it, mumbles something to the assistant still on the phone, and then closes the door, locking it.

"Speak. What the fuck are you talking about?" he asks in a loud whisper.

"Stop," I say. "I know. I've known from the start."

He crosses the floor in two seconds and gets nose-to-nose with me. "What is it you think you know, Mitchell? I can assure you that you don't know shit."

I hold up my hands like I'm in a bank that's being robbed. "I don't know everything, but I know it was Lucy that killed Murphy Beckett, OK? I know about her husband. Maybe a couple of those other guys all those months back. I also know you know, and I know you hid it."

Aaron inhales deeply through his nose and glares at me for several seconds as a clock ticks on his desk. It was a gift from the mayor of a small town in the county when Aaron was elected. We listen to it and stare at each other, Aaron's shoulders moving in time with the ragged breath blowing through his nostrils. There's indecision in his eyes as he grits his teeth.

"How long?" he finally asks.

I shrug and squint. "How long what?"

"How long have you known, Mitchell?"

I steel my shoulders. He could fire me, but that'd be stupid. No. Aaron Dwyer is stuck with me for the rest of his life, and I'm stuck with him now. We're in this shit together.

"Before Beckett even died." I leave out the part about killers knowing their own.

He blinks. Twice. "You knew that long? I didn't even know until much later."

I raise an eyebrow. "That's interesting. When did you figure it out?"

His ears redden, the color from his face moving there, and I can't deny that I like that I may be the bumbling guy every-one overlooks, but I figured out everything faster than Aaron Dwyer.

"I won't tell you the details," he says through gritted teeth. "I'm interested in your starting point."

"Since we started surveilling the club before Murphy died. We knew drugs were moving through there. It was too conve-nient that your girl moved from Chicago, had ties to Beckett, her abusive husband was missing, and the missing husband was involved with the dead mafia bodies. I assume she killed her ex-husband and that's why nobody brings his case up. Honestly, I'm kind of disappointed you didn't suspect her earlier. Hell, at one point, I thought you were in on it. I thought for sure you offed the ex."

I thought that because that's what I would have done.

He grits his teeth until I think they'll crack before releasing his jaw, rolling his shoulders, and blowing out a deep breath.

"Wait. *Did* you off the ex?" I ask, dropping my chin and smirking. "Your secret is safe with me."

"I didn't kill him, but I'm blind to many things about my wife. Always have been. Always will be."

"It's Cheryl."

"What?" Dwyer asks, squinting even deeper until the lines between his eyes show and shaking his head a bit.

"The person killing off all the dudes in town right now. It's Cheryl. She didn't kill that county treasurer, though," I hold up a finger. I need to make that part clear. "That doesn't fit her style, and she doesn't have the physical strength to string a guy up like that. Whoever did him is probably long gone and not even local."

Aaron rears back, and I almost expect him to throw a punch. But it's shock this time. He tilts his head like it's finally coming together in his brain. Cheryl's missing ex is so much like Lucy's situation, and then there are the dead bad guys that rolled through Peter's club.

He opens and closes his mouth twice as he finds the words. "Honestly, I thought it was Lucy again. Well, except for the county treasurer. I know she wouldn't fuck with that kind of press exposure. You're telling me it's *not* Lucy?"

My eyes widen, and I whistle. "Damn. You thought your wife was killing again and you were still going to let it slide? Ballsy. I can respect that, though. That's why I'm here to ensure our mutual destruction if one of us goes down. But no, sir. It's not Lucy. It's my girl this time."

He closes his eyes and falls back into the guest chair behind him. I'm glad I didn't move it when I fell into it the first time. He takes for granted it's there to catch him. I've known him a few years, and it's humbling to see the relief on his face.

Holy shit. He really thought Lucy was on the rampage, and he wasn't going to breathe a word. He was going to cover for her again.

"You really weren't going to let her go down for any more crime, huh? You must love that woman."

He bites the inside of his cheek and looks at the floor. "She's pregnant."

I nod. "Congratulations are in order then."

"I thought it was hormones or something. She hasn't felt well the last couple weeks." Leaning forward, he hangs his head, defeated. "Tell me what happened."

"Cheryl killed her ex, Daniel Martin. It was an accident after he attacked her. Self-defense. You know how you'd feel if it was Lucy. I figured that much out. After we had a chat about it, she explained everything. Turns out, your wife helped her out afterward since it happened in her parking lot. She won't tell me where the body is."

"If my wife helped hide the body, I have an idea," he says. He then mumbles something like, "Fucking Ellen." I have no idea what that means, and Dwyer must understand that from my expression. He sighs. "Ellen owns the campground where we found Portsmith. That's why I thought it was Lucy. I thought she went back to her old stomping grounds."

My eyes widen as the light bulb goes off over my head. "That's why you didn't want to drag the pond. There's something in there you think will connect to Lucy."

He nods. "She basically dissolved her ex and put what was left in the pond. It was very little, but I couldn't risk it. That pond will never be dragged as long as I'm the sheriff of this county."

"Cheryl killed Acox, Portsmith, and her ex, but she didn't off Ricord. Like I said, I don't know who killed him."

I don't own up to that kill with Dwyer. Protecting my girl is one thing. Outing myself as a vicious killer in another. I'm only in Dwyer's office to protect Cheryl now. Lucy for Cheryl makes us even. Throw me in and it's no longer tit for tat. Dwyer can empathize with me protecting my girl, but he won't have the stomach for me going vigilante.

"I saw the CCTV footage of Cheryl baiting Portsmith," I continue. "I thought about how what happened with Lucy hasn't happened again. I mean, Lucy's reign of terror was obviously isolated. Something with the mafia, I'm guessing, and it stopped after she handled it. You probably know more." I hold up my hands. "I'll never ask you for the details. But Cheryl, well, she has a taste for it. There's something in her head, man." I point to my temple. "I know she was hurt, probably like Lucy was hurt by her ex-husband, and I know you understand. I just think your girl needed to kill to get out of a bad situation. My girl? A bad situation made *her* the bad situation. I guess that happens when you push women too far. They *will* strike back, and when you finally wake the beast, the chips will fall and heads will roll, even if it takes a long time for the shit rain to fall on everyone who deserves it."

"What are you going to do?" he asks.

I have no intention of telling my boss that a few of the kills in the county Coleson has investigated over the last two years are really mine. Taking Lucy's kills and Cheryl's kills out of the equation, there's only one murder in this county in the last two years that I can't take credit for.

One in the entire county that can be chalked up to random.

First, I'm going to continue acting dumb at work to keep a low profile. Second, I'm going to leverage his girl's past to keep mine safe, and then we're all going to stop killing people until the next big dickhead comes along. One of us will handle the business when a shit stain thinks he can fuck around with the innocent people of this county, and the rest of us will rally around them while Aaron Dwyer keeps his mouth shut.

I lean back against his desk. "I never spoke a word about Lucy, even when I knew you took that hair sample out." He lifts his head and sets his jaw. I hold up a hand, hopeful he won't grip my throat again. "By the way, brilliant move getting Foster to retire and hiring Avery. Nothing causes evidence and casework to fall to the wayside like staff turnover. Too bad Avery is smarter than anyone gives her credit for. We'll have to be careful around her, and that's why I'm here. She's smart as fuck and will figure this out if we let her. Honestly, boss, you could have hired someone incompetent like Foster, but you just had to go and hire a capable woman who will hold our feet to the fire if we slip up. Dumb. She's not interested in joining the boys' club, and I bet you thought she was young and malleable."

I've toyed with getting rid of Avery somehow, but I can't. I don't harm innocent people, and I can't help but like her. In fact, I'd be honored if she was the one to find out what I am. It would be like a rookie basketball player dunking on Michael Jordan back in the nineties. You can't be mad at it.

I also can't be mad because I see something in her, too. There's something about her that screams to me that she may not be so quick to turn me in if she figured out my side hobby. Maybe it's the bravado or something else I can't put into words, but she also has the darkness. At least, she has the capability for it. Whether she's ever used it or ever would, I can't be sure.

I smile as Dwyer turns everything over in his mind. "I know everything, and that includes the hair. That day when I was talking to you about the cases? The day you asked Lucy to marry you? I knew. I was trying to get you to slip up. It didn't work. Your only goal was marrying Lucy. That's why I'm here. I'm sorry I broke it to you the way I did. I didn't mean to sound like I was challenging you. I just really need advice."

"About what?"

"I want to marry Cheryl, and I want us to agree to protect our wives."

"Like an alliance?" he asks.

"Yes."

"You just met her. You don't have the history I have with Lucy. Cut free. Walk away."

"I can't. I love her. I may not have the years of history you do with Lucy, but my love for Cheryl is strong. I can't walk away. I won't leave those boys. I'm going to have a future with her. Defiantly. Stupidly. But I'm going to be with her for the rest of my life."

"That may not be very long. Lucy killed in self-defense. If Cheryl has a taste for it, you could be in danger if you break her heart."

Fat chance of that. Fear of death works both ways in our relationship. But we both only kill shitty people. Always have. We won't hurt innocents. We simply hate bullies. We'll also keep our family and friends safe.

"Well, I'll just have to be on my best behavior now, won't I?" I tap my toes against the worn carpet and cross my arms. "She only kills the bad guys. I'm going to marry her and take care of her so she doesn't have to do that anymore. I can make it stop if I can make her feel safe."

He leans back in his seat and adjusts the tie at his neck. "You can't save her, man. She has to want to stop by herself."

"We'll see. Are you going to turn her in?"

A laugh bubbles from his chest, and he smiles a maniacal grin befitting a movie villain before shaking his head. "These women really have us by the balls, don't they?"

"What do you mean?"

"You love Cheryl and won't rat her out. I love my wife and won't let her spend a second in a jail cell, especially not when she's carrying my child. You know about Lucy, and now I know about Cheryl. We can't tell on each other because then the other will go down. It's a real fucking mess here. All along, I thought it was just me and Lucy, but you knew. You say you knew and didn't tell on her."

I nod. "Yeah. I didn't and I won't. I know you may not believe this, but I respect what she did, and I respect what you did to protect her."

That's putting it mildly. Lucy Dwyer was a badass genius not one person saw coming and solved a lot of problems in this county. She probably saved a lot of lives by killing a drug and human trafficker, not to mention the mafia trash she took out.

I look at the wall behind Dwyer and wonder how many lives I've saved over time. How many potential sexual assault victims don't know the horror of it because I handled my special business? A sly smile forms at the corner of my mouth at the thought of women being able to sleep better at night.

I'm nobody's hero, but like I told Cheryl, I'm a solid antihero. That's enough for now.

"Then I won't tell on Cheryl." He straightens his face and glares at me. "This isn't me being nice to her. This is me still protecting Lucy, and I'll protect Lucy until my dying breath."

"I'll protect Cheryl the same way. If Coleson or anyone else comes sniffing, we need to have a united front. That's why I'm telling you. We're better if we're a team. We can protect them better if we work together."

Dwyer puts his head in his hands for a moment and then swipes his fingers down his face, leaving red marks. I stand to leave because I'm a serial killer. That means I'm great with nonverbal communication. He's annoyed, and I've dropped enough shit sandwiches in his lap for the day. He needs to center himself and realize the depth of our conversation, and he needs to do that alone.

I nod as I leave, still showing respect for my boss. "I'll be out on patrol if you need me."

"Alright. We aren't blackmailing each other about this, right?"

I'm halfway to the door, but I freeze and spin to face him. "No, sir. That's not my intention here."

And it's not. I just needed to dangle Lucy's indiscretions in front of him so Cheryl won't ever be pinned for what she's done. I'm not out to hurt Aaron and Lucy. Aaron Dwyer is a decent man, and Lucy was just like me for a span of a few months. If anything, I'd have her back if someone took a pop at her.

"So, there's nothing you want to hold over me?"

I smile and turn on the clueless deputy charm. "Can I have a promotion?"

Dwyer smirks. "You'll make a hell of a detective someday if we ever get funding to have two on staff in our little county. Hell, if your girl keeps fileting shitty men, the council may put it in the budget. Or, we could have to get rid of positions since all the shit men in town will be fucking dead." He chuckles. "We need to get our girls under control or we'll all be out of jobs. I expect we'll never speak of this again unless it's to protect one of them. Do we understand each other?"

"Yes, sir."

I spin toward the door again and give him a stiff wave over my shoulder because we do understand each other. I think we *all* understand what needs to be done to protect the women we love.

But I *am* like Aaron Dwyer in one way...

I pat the little box in my pocket that seems so foreign there. It's next to my favorite knife, and my pants feel bulky with the weight of both objects. I've been carrying it around for two days, waiting until Cheryl is off work and we can spend time together, but I'm ready to get the ring out of my pocket and on her finger where it belongs. Now I know where the term about something burning a hole in a pocket comes from.

I'm going to do what I can to clean up any evidence here, and then I'm going to go straight home and ask Cheryl Briggs to be my wife. I'm going to be the best stepfather I can be to those boys, and I'll have a family with the woman I love more than anything or anyone. She may be a serial killer, but she's *mine*.

And I'm hers.

If someone gets in the way of that, I'll fucking deal with it. Or Cheryl will. Hell, maybe Lucy will come out of retirement. I guess we'll see.

THE END

***

Thanks for reading *Bang*. I hope you enjoyed it. Make sure to leave a star rating or review on your reading platform.

If you'd like to keep up with when I have a new release, you can follow me on Bookbub or follow me on Instagram or Facebook at @authortoriross.

Again, a sincere thanks from the bottom of my heart. I appreciate my readers, and the best thing you can do to help me if you enjoy this story/series is tell a friend.

Also by Tori Ross

Romantic Suspense

Copper

Bang

***

Polyamory Romance

Disco Bar

***

Romantic Comedy

All I Wank for Christmas

The Panty Plot

The Sole Scheme – Coming Soon

The Cuffing Season Contract
Contact High
Baked and Burned

***

Contemporary Shorts
Rocks

***

Superhero Romance
Arson
Thirst
Darkness
Amp

Acknowledgements

This shit again. This section is the hardest part of writing a book for me. That and coming up with the playlist on Spotify, which I spend way too much time doing when I sit down to write books.

At this point, I think I've thanked my husband about a million times, but the long-suffering bastard doesn't get nearly as much praise as he should. He gives me time to write, encourages me, and thinks all of this is cool AF. Thanks, Travis. I honestly could not be married to any other poor soul.

To my kids, A and P, who also listen to the most random plot points and author problems at the dinner table. They also help me name characters, and my oldest is the best event PA money can buy. (Spoiler, she works for free.)

Thank you to Lisa, Kristie, the Lauras from porch drinking, Paige, Chrissy, Jaime, Jess, Nicole N, and I'm sure I'm forgetting someone else in my real life who supports my books and chosen side hustle, even if it's just a text or social media comment that you're proud of me. For this book, I'm going to also thank my beginning improv class over at The Improv Shop in St. Louis. They kept the creative juices flowing. Even though this book was not a comedy, class helped me break up my boring weeks of writing murder scenes and kept the creative part of my brain set to "On."

Outside of real life, a big thanks to my author friends who either give me a shoutout or just let me cry on their shoulders with messages asking, "Can you believe this bullshit?": Evie, Selena, Adonia, Kelly, Christian, Samantha, Indie, and EL. Thank you to my fellow mods over at the Cinnamon Roll Book Boyfriends Facebook group.

Thank you to Deb and April, my proofreaders on rotating projects.

I have to thank my dogs, Meyer and Murphy. They always know just when Mom needs a writing break and will come over and relentlessly paw at me until I get up. Mostly, I just think they want a pup cup.

Lastly, thank you to the people who enjoyed *Copper*. You're why *Bang* exists because *Copper* was always meant to be a stand-alone. *Bang* wasn't even in my writing schedule and just kind of "happened" in November of 2024. Thank you for being here.

About Tori Ross

Tori Ross is an Amazon bestselling and Apple Top 100 author. Her book, *The Cuffing Season Contract*, won the National Indie Excellence Award for romantic comedy, and *Disco Bar* was a Passionate Plume finalist in the steamy category. She lives with her family and two rescue dogs in the Midwest.